The Scrapbook of Sherlock Holmes

Archie Rushden

First edition published in 2016
© Copyright 2016
Archie Rusdhen

The right of Archie Rushden to be identified as the author of this work has been asserted by him in accordance with the Copyright, Designs and Patents Act 1998.

All rights reserved. No reproduction, copy or transmission of this publication may be made without express prior written permission. No paragraph of this publication may be reproduced, copied or transmitted except with express prior written permission or in accordance with the provisions of the Copyright Act 1956 (as amended). Any person who commits any unauthorized act in relation to this publication may be liable to criminal prosecution and civil claims for damage.

All characters appearing in this work are fictitious. Any resemblance to real persons, living or dead, is purely coincidental. The opinions expressed herein are those of the authors and not of MX Publishing.

Paperback ISBN 978-1-78092-921-7
ePub ISBN 978-1-78092-922-4
PDF ISBN 978-1-78092-923-1

Published in the UK by MX Publishing
335 Princess Park Manor, Royal Drive, London, N11 3GX
www.mxpublishing.com
Cover design by www.staunch.com

To my favourite Tenor Horn, Trombone, and Euphonium

Contents

Introduction	1
The Adventure of The Weeping Man	3
The Case of the Angry American	15
The Adventure of the Spurned Lover	28
The Augean Stables	42
The Affair of the involuntary Spy	52
The Case of the bewildered Banker	67
The Case of the Holy Bones	82
The Affair of the Silver Bandsman	98
The Affair of the Missing Passenger	113
The Steam Yacht *Pegasus*	126

' "…Make a long arm, Watson, and see what V has to say."

I leaned back and took down the great volume to which he referred. Holmes balanced it in his knee and his eyes moved slowly and lovingly over the record of old cases, mixed with the accumulated information of a lifetime.'

The Adventure of the Sussex Vampire

Introduction

A year ago, a quite remarkable discovery was made at Charing Cross Station in London. In the course of minor building work, associated with the relocation of automatic ticket machines, a brick wall beside the left luggage office was demolished.

Behind the wall was found a number of items of left or lost luggage, which had evidently fallen into a space between the newly demolished wall and high fitted cupboards or shelves from the old lost property store. Amongst the abandoned umbrellas, gloves and hats was a large whicker hamper, which bore the tantalising label "CC Underground: Nov 11th 1918."

The contents of the hamper, though largely typical of the material usually lost or left on the underground railway, were of some interest as a 'snapshot' of one day's business for the lost property department. The fact that the one day happened also to be Armistice Day, when the guns of the Great War finally fell silent, was an added bonus.

The significance of the day was not lost on the 'historians' of the railway either and several items were passed without delay to the Museum of London. These included a khaki service cap, complete with Machine Gun Corps badge, and several special editions of local and national newspapers. Oddest of all was a German Iron Cross medal, presumably a soldier's souvenir, and an artificial hand; also perhaps a sad relic of the war.

Two items were retained by the railway. One was a file from the Ministry of Munitions, which was eventually returned to Parliament for appraisal before transfer to the National Archives. The other was a leather attaché case, bearing the inscription 'Dr J H W'.

The attaché case was clearly much used but of good quality. It contained a sheaf of typescript papers, clipped

1

together, and a couple of inconsequential notes and circulars; the notes mostly on the headed paper of a general hospital unit of the Royal Army Medical Corps. Sadly, there was neither address nor signature to confirm the ownership of the case.

On further examination, the typescript papers proved to be the most remarkable find of all and suggestive – if not actual proof – of their owner's identity. If they really are what they purport to be (and archival analysis is currently being carried out) then the building work at Charing Cross may have revealed a literary find of no small significance. Nothing less, in fact, than a cache of lost cases of Sherlock Holmes, penned by his 'Boswell', the redoubtable Dr John H Watson.

The Adventure of the Weeping Man

I would not describe my friend Mr Sherlock Holmes as a secretive man. That so much of his early life and his family remained unknown to the few of us privileged to be able to call him a friend, was due more to his preoccupation with the business of the present than a disinclination to recall the past.

On the rare occasions when Holmes's mood did turn to reminiscence, you may imagine then with what eagerness I greeted his every word. Occasionally, a biographical titbit would be deployed in order to divert me from some course of action upon which I had set my heart, such as a campaign against his more noxious chemical experimentation, but I knew better than to interrupt my friend when he was recalling past events. Instead, I would seize my pen or pencil and listen.

I recollect one such evening, a couple of years before my marriage. It was in the autumn, I think, of 1886. Torrential rain, which still blurred our windows, had kept us both indoors and the aching of an old wound (a souvenir of service in Afghanistan) made me an ill-tempered companion. Holmes and I sat, engulfed by an oppressive silence for several hours. I irritably flapped the pages of my newspaper at him, while he blew and whistled through a blocked briar pipe at me.

At length I decided upon a complete change for my wounded shoulder's sake and I flopped onto an elderly chaise-longue, which our housekeeper, Mrs Hudson, had recently seen fit to introduce into our sitting room. I must confess that I threw myself down rather heavily and may quite possibly have driven the couch an inch or two backwards into a tall pile of files which Holmes had unwisely stowed between it and the wall. I was immediately deluged, almost buried, in an avalanche of dusty and cob-webbed cardboard and foolscap.

Holmes and I stared at one another for fully a minute. Then he sprang to his feet with a cry of "Ha! Excellent Watson! How often do you reveal what eludes me?" Holmes was beside me in two steps and snatched from the pile spread across my stomach a long, thin, blue paper folded lengthways in half.

"But Holmes," I protested, more out of form than conviction, "these papers of yours are filthy and their pile cannot have been stable if I could bring it down merely by…"

"Quite so, Watson" interrupted Holmes. "You have toppled my topless tower but more to the point, you have unearthed a precious relic of my first case as a private consulting detective."

"Your first case?" I gasped.

"Well, my first *paid* case at least."

"My dear Holmes," I replied, "I should be pleased to add some details of that case to the slight record I have been able to compile of…"

"So you shall my dear Watson. I see though that the rain has, at last stopped and I suspect we would both benefit from a stroll in the fresh, new-washed air. Perhaps I can beguile you with my memories as we walk?"

With barely a backward glance at the piles of papers cascading across our furniture and floor, I seized my hat and coat, and dashed after Holmes, whose clattering boots were already two thirds of the way down the stairs to our front door.

Ordinarily, a stroll with Holmes swiftly became an exploration of that web of narrow courts and alleyways which lie behind our capital's great thoroughfares like the lesser capillaries between our veins and arteries. This time however, we marched arm in arm along the Marylebone and

Euston Roads as far as Gower Street. I walked in silence, knowing better than to attempt to begin our conversation. Holmes had enticed me out and would commence when he was ready.

Finally, we halted before the gates and courtyard of University College. Holmes pointed at the colonnade with his stick.

"There was a time, my dear Watson, when I knew very little of London besides the few streets between this courtyard and my lodgings in Montague Street."

"You set up there as a detective?" I asked.

"No, no, Watson, I came first as a student."

"Then you were not at Oxford or Cambridge? I had assumed…"

"Ah, Watson, neither of the 'old' universities were entirely suitable for a nonconformist in those days", Holmes replied with a chuckle, "in either sense of the word."

"You were not happy in the Church of England then?" I asked.

"It was my upbringing Watson; habit rather than conviction. There was a Swedenborgian chapel behind the Charing Cross Road then, which formed the third point of a rather triangular existence. Do you recall my mentioning my friend Victor Trevor? It was my unseemly haste, not to be late for that chapel, which excited his terrier enough to savage my ankle. The dog was a brute but Trevor became the only real friend of a particularly miserable period of my life."

My companion paused then, his face clearly showing that he was reliving that bleak period, of poverty and loneliness. At length Holmes rallied and turned his thin smile towards me.

"But my dear Watson, I have promised you a memoir of those long-gone days". Holmes tapped the pavement twice with his stick. "My story begins here. You have several times noted, with flattering wonder in your narratives of my slender achievements, that I have some slight skill in observation and interpretation of that observation. Well, Watson, I first began to exploit that ability here, as an entertainment for my friend Victor Trevor."

"Every Friday we would conclude our week's studies with an omnibus ride into the West End and an evening of music or drama. Our tastes were catholic and we would spend our few spare pennies on the music hall one week and seats at the rear of Covent Garden's 'gods' the next. It was a ritual we enjoyed and one of the few compensations we knew."

"One evening I astonished Trevor by identifying every passenger ascending the turning stair of our 'bus by his or her trade or calling. You know my trick Watson; a discharged soldier by his bearing and boots, a printer by his cuffs and a sweep by his ears. He was delighted and it became quite my 'party trick'; something that Trevor would always request whenever we boarded the Friday evening 'bus."

Regularly therefore we would take up the seats at the rear of the 'bus, where we could best observe our fellow travellers. On the evening in question (a beautiful, sunny, summer evening) I was accompanying Trevor not to the theatre but to Liverpool Street Station, from whence he was to catch a train home for the weekend. For most of the journey we were alone inside, until an elderly fellow who was – to our embarrassment – convulsed in tearful sobs as though burdened by the deepest of misfortune boarded the 'bus."

"Trevor and I looked in astonishment at one another. Concluding that the poor chap was best left alone with his tears, we turned instead to our sport. Truly, Watson, I excelled myself. There was a fishmonger (too easy!) a librarian and a nursemaid – whose charges (though absent) I asserted were a boy of four or five, a babe in arms, and a girl with long red hair. There were other passengers but alas I cannot now recall the full extent of my tawdry triumph."

"At length we reached Liverpool Street and I waved farewell to my friend. I strolled out of the station, eager for my evening on the town, and ran almost immediately and all too literally, into the weeping man from the omnibus. To my utter astonishment the old fellow wasn't at all put out. Indeed, he seemed delighted and gripped my coat with a firmness which surprised me."

"My dear young sir", he gasped out in a reedy voice. "I am in desperate need and I fancy yours is the very skill I need. You must be heaven sent sir! Truly you must!"

"Well, Watson, I tried to detach him from my lapels but he would have none of it. We waltzed about the station's *porte-cochère* until I agreed to join him for a drink in the buffet. There he told me his tale of woe and why my rare skill was of such interest to him."

"The poor fellow was a dairyman, Watson, by the name of Rudge; as prosperous and easy-going a man as any in his home town of Kilmerton in Suffolk. He'd begun with nothing beyond a barrow, a churn of milk and a set of copper measures. Years of hard work, bolstered by a cheery manner and unfailing honesty, had rewarded him with money enough to contemplate a contented retirement, happy in the society of numerous friends and a loving wife and daughter."

"Then came the kidnapper."

"The kidnapper!" I exclaimed. "But who was abducted? Surely not the daughter?"

"Indeed Watson, it was the daughter. A poor child of barely sixteen. With eyes so weak that she might easily have been taken for blind. Such are the cruelties of the world."

"Did this Rudge not go to the police?" I asked.

"Of course," replied my friend, "and not without success. First he sought the aid of the Suffolk force and then came for detectives from Scotland Yard."

"You say 'not without success', I asked with some nervousness, fearing for the abducted child.

"Exactly, Watson" Holmes responded. "The Scotland Yarders set their trap and soon sprung it, seizing a particularly loathsome specimen, who declined to give away even his own name, let alone the whereabouts of the missing daughter. Believe me Watson it was a devilish predicament. The police had the kidnapper but the kidnapper had the daughter. He made it plain too that the helpless blind girl would soon die, if he were not released in time to save her."

"Poor Rudge was at his wits' end. How long can a young girl last without food and water? The abductor had been arrested as he collected five hundred pounds (the dairyman's life-savings) from a hollow tree beside the road from Ipswich to Kilmerton and had been already more than twelve hours in custody. I tell you Watson, neither Rudge nor the police could see any alternative to releasing the rogue. They were stumped."

"Then, on his journey back to the station hotel, Rudge had seen my little trick of identification and had seen a chink of light dispelling his gloom. We hastened to Scotland Yard by cab and within half an hour I was sitting opposite the abductor in his cell."

"I felt revulsion at first Watson. Believe me, the fellow was evil – of that there was no doubt – but within a few minutes my interest was aroused and pure deductive power, untainted by emotion or feelings, reigned supreme. I flatter myself too, Watson, that within five minutes the case was solved – save for shoe leather and physical energy."

"The man who sat opposite me in that cell was a small, sallow faced creature, clean-shaven save for a fringe of whisker from ear to ear around his chin. He grinned at me, revealing a row of even, yellow, tobacco-stained teeth. He had icy blue eyes, which danced and twinkled with malice, even though one was now surrounded with a most impressive bruise. The villain took in that I had noticed the black-eye and smiled even more broadly."

"The rozzers helped me to this," he declared bitterly, "they thought it might loosen my tongue but I shan't say a word more'n I want now. They can do what they like but they can't hang a man for murder without a body. No evidence, see? That's as I sees it anyhow."

"It is murder then?" I replied, "I thought we were considering a case of abduction and false imprisonment."

"Think what you like. If I don't leave 'ere soon with five hundred in sovereigns and no one following me, it'll be murder for certain."

"All this time, Watson, I was studying the fellow. His boots were particularly interesting, believe me. At length I asked him to stand and turn about for me. He did so with a leer, as though I were a fool to be humoured. I had seen what I needed though and finally offered the repulsive animal my hand, as though in gratitude for his forbearance. This amused him even more and he cocked an eye at the policeman who attended us and chuckled as though to add me to his list of the defeated. Finally, I reached across and picked a stray fibre from the sleeve of his rough tweed jacket."

"Rudge and an Inspector Baldwin (who seethed with barely suppressed rage) awaited me outside the cell."

"Must we release him, Mr Holmes?" asked Rudge.

"By no means" I replied. "But we must hurry. Inspector, have you any paper and a pen and ink I might use?"

"We were taken back down a dimly-lit corridor to the inspector's office, where I sat at his desk and composed a brief message…on the very slip of Metropolitan Police paper which you unearthed, Watson, a few hours ago."

"What did you write?" I asked eagerly.

"It was a simple message, with instructions. See for yourself, Watson," said Holmes, taking the blue folded paper from his pocket and handing it back to me. I unfolded it and read my friend's familiar writing beneath the printed Scotland Yard heading:

Telegraph this to every vicarage or rectory within twenty miles of Kilmerton.

Is your sexton at home?

Reply Chief Constable, Ipswich.
S. Holmes

"You see Watson, the fellow had told me all I needed, not in words but in clues which were just as readable. We then left Scotland Yard for the railway station and an express to Ipswich."

By this time Holmes and I had reached the British Museum. We walked along beside the railings, Holmes meditatively running his stick along them as we walked; a thoughtful smile playing across his lips.

"I imagine," said I, "that the Ipswich police were bombarded with telegraphic replies and eager for an explanation when you arrived."

"Indeed they were Watson but a few words from Inspector Baldwin smoothed their ruffled feathers and within ten minutes we had as committed a set of allies as ever I've been associated with."

"The last telegram arrived at about ten the next morning, leaving only two sextons unaccounted for. We set out immediately for the nearest parish by fly, hired from the railway station. It proved a false trail. The fool of a clergyman had taken our appeal all too literally and reported his sexton 'missing' from home, even though he was actually widely known to have been admitted only that week to the poor law infirmary with an injured back."

"So, Watson, we hastened on to the more remote parish. It was a tiny place called Remisham Prior; barely more than half a dozen houses, the rectory and a Norman church squeezed up against the high brick wall of a Jacobean manor house."

"There we struck gold! A few words of description to the rector were enough for him to identify the villain in custody as Thornton Slade, his sexton and a sly malcontent at the root of half the trouble which ever afflicted that lonely hamlet."

"Of course the police wasted no time in battering in the door of Slade's hovel but they found no girl there. We searched his garden, stoving-in two barrels and a brick cucumber frame to no benefit. His shed, in the corner of the churchyard, proved equally empty – save for a shovel, spade and a wooden frame in the shape of an over-size coffin. A search of the church, an interesting example of plain Norman architecture, was similarly unproductive. There was simply no-where to hide a girl, save in the cupboard-like vestry but that held nothing more suspicious than a mildewed cassock and a hat-box full of half-burnt candles."

"In vain I tried to comfort poor Rudge. In truth Watson, I needed to think and to be alone to do it, so I did not attempt to dissuade either the distraught father or my police escort when they proposed a pointless search of the neighbouring fields."

"I retired to Thornton Slade's shed, where I sat upon an up-turned bucket and smoked my way through nearly half a pouch of tobacco. With my eyes closed, I revisited in my mind every inch of Slade's cottage and garden. There was nowhere we had not examined. I mentally searched once more the little church, from font to apse; lime-washed chantry chapel to bell-cote. There was nothing! And yet, Watson, there **had** to be somewhere else. I could not be mistaken!"

"Ah, but then Watson, I had the answer! I ran as fast as I could back to the churchyard, where, in an extension screened by the wall of the Jacobean house and a row of stubby yews, was the 'mausoleum' of the family which had held the manor from the Dissolution. It was a stone vault, with a front deliberately fashioned to resemble a cave entrance, sealed with heavy iron doors."

"I examined the lock and you may imagine my delight, Watson, when I found minute, shiny scratches across metal which should by rights have been green with age and weather. I battered my fists against those doors and pressed my ear against the lock. I fancied that I heard movement within."

"Neither respect for the deceased occupants nor their living relatives deterred me then Watson, as I tore back to Slade's hovel. I wasted fully ten minutes in a fruitless search for the key but then abandoned the hunt, returning to the 'mausoleum' armed with a chisel and hammer. A further five minutes passed before I was able to enter and emerge again, the poor, blind victim of Thornton Slade's depravity in my arms!"

"Remarkable, Holmes!" I cried. "This is a tale worthy of Poe or Le Fanu. Why is it not already well known?"

"Why? Watson," replied my friend, his expression full of ironic amusement. Partly from consideration for the poor girl herself and in part, I suppose, because I was given money to remain silent. Remember, Watson, it was my first **paid** case."

"But Holmes, why on earth would Rudge pay you to remain silent? And how could he keep the newspapers from reporting so astounding a trial – in which you must surely have made your name as a witness."

"There was no trial, Watson, because Rudge lost his nerve and telegraphed Scotland Yard to release Slade with his five hundred sovereigns and free passage. Rudge and his policemen returned with news of the girl's hiding place barely an hour after I had released her. We parted on ill terms and though I was disgusted with his folly I was also fifteen guineas the richer. That modest sum representing, in those days, both my professional fee and the price of my silence. I can add that despite the best efforts of both Scotland Yard and the Suffolk constabulary, Thornton Slade was never again heard of – at least by that name."

"So, there, Watson, you have an account of my first professional work; though it will avail you not a whit, as I fear my oath of silence still holds good. Come, I rather fancy (from the scents emanating from her kitchen as we left) that Mrs Hudson has been preparing one of her sustaining steak and kidney puddings! We must not be late and, in any case, reliving this affair of the weeping man has engendered quite an appetite."

We turned then back towards Baker Street and our dinner, abandoning the principal thoroughfares to thread our way through the secret routes so beloved of my friend. We were stepping around a broad, oily puddle in the centre of the dismal Half-Moon Court, when I suddenly realised that I still lacked the central feature of Holmes's tale. I gripped his arm.

"Holmes," I asked earnestly, "how did you know Slade was a sexton and why within twenty miles of Kilmerton?"

"Come Watson, isn't it obvious? I sized the odious fellow up. I shook his hand, which was calloused and grimed from manual, earthy labour. I picked a fibre from many on his sleeve of hempen bell-rope and I saw his boots. Many labourers will have soil on their boots but few will have signs of every layer of soil from grass and top-soil to the clay of six feet down. His jacket was smeared with powdery white lime wash, there were traces of cobwebs by the flap of his pocket and there was coal or coke dust on his fraying cuff. Come, Watson, who else digs deep holes, shovels coal, rings bells and generally lives in a world of lime-wash and spider's webs?"

"That he was a sexton then was easily deduced. Or so it seemed in the confidence of youth. As for the twenty miles, well, I suppose that I reasoned on some local knowledge, or transmission of a story of Rudge's retirement and modest wealth, yet distance enough that the rogue wasn't known to him and recognised. Besides, a longer distance would not have been practicable. One should not cast a net too widely. "

Holmes smiled and offered me his hand, as I stretched out over the scummed pool: "Perhaps I should not be so confident in my deductions today but time was pressing and what choice had I?"

The Case of the Angry American

In all the years of my association with Mr Sherlock Holmes, I can recall only three cases in which my friend's involvement came as a result of an intervention from the perpetrator of the crime. Many villains imagine their schemes to be fool-proof, otherwise they would hardly embark upon them, but even so, it is a rarity when they deliberately involve the police or (yet more dangerously) a detective with the reputation of Mr Sherlock Holmes.

My notes reveal only one case however, in which the evil-doer drew upon himself my friend's attention wholly by mistake. It was a particularly hot evening, in the summer of 1889. Holmes and I were seated, beside the open window of our rooms in Baker Street, deriving some small relief from the heat of the day, from the slight breeze which almost imperceptibly disturbed our lace curtains.

I remember that Holmes almost lay in his chair, a slight smile on his lips and his eyes quite closed. I was working at my pipe, which seemed determined not to 'draw' to my satisfaction. Nevertheless, it was Holmes who reacted first, leaping to his feet and seizing our poker, when suddenly our door was flung open and a huge figure burst in upon us.

Our visitor stood silently in our doorway, almost completely obscuring poor Mrs Hudson, behind him, who had vainly attempted to prevent the invasion. For fully a minute we eyed each other, Holmes still clutching the poker, while I searched our rooms desperately with my eyes for a weapon. The intruder merely breathed heavily and held steady a large revolver, which he had only partially raised from his waistband.

"We-e-ell," drawled our visitor at last, "it seems we all know what'll happen if we don't just settle peaceably for a parley." His speech betrayed a deal of scant-suppressed anger and I was all the more astonished when Sherlock Holmes replied civilly that perhaps a drink would help on so hot a night and that Mrs Hudson might withdraw. I sat back into my chair, with a quiet wish that Mrs Hudson would immediately seek the aid of a constable.

Holmes however, remained quietly hospitable. He proffered a glass of whisky and soda to our huge intruder, lightly adding "I fear you have us at a disadvantage. I am Sherlock Holmes and this is my friend and colleague, Dr Watson. Pray take a seat. Is it to one or both of us that you address yourself?"

The giant lurched two steps into the room, seeming to tower over my friend, who had resumed his chair.

"You can keep your drink! I am not yet sure whether I shall shoot you or simply crack your head open."

"Well," responded Holmes, "while you consider your best course of action, I would ask you to introduce yourself."

"You know me well enough!" replied our visitor, dashing Holmes's proffered glass aside. "Don't try to hog-tie me with fancy words and cut glass. I am in no mood for speechifying, nor cake-walking around the subject. I have come to say one thing to you, Mr Sherlock Holmes the detective. Get out of my business! Stay out of it and leave that thief Valdes to me! If not, well…well" and here his eyes ranged about our room, "I might not be so careful what I puncture next time!" He then drew his impressive revolver and fired three deafening shots into my portrait of General Gordon, resplendent in Egyptian uniform and tarboosh, which slipped first to one side and then another before falling forwards onto our sideboard.

I sprang to my feet but Holmes gestured that I should stay my hand. Our visitor gazed for a moment at the thick bluish smoke as it issued from his revolver and then, smilingly, returned it to his trousers.

"The dude in the flower-pot this time," he smirked, "you two *gentlemen* are next, if I have to draw again! Stay out of my affairs!" He then whirled about in the doorway and almost flew down our stairs, slamming shut the door as he went.

Holmes made no attempt to follow but rather hastened to our window for a moment or two, before returning our poker to the grate.

"Well, well," he said cheerily, "we pined for a breeze and we reaped a whirlwind. I wonder what the fellow wanted. He wasn't a wronged husband in search of you was he, Watson?"

"He was not!" I replied indignantly. "Besides, he addressed himself quite clearly to you. I know nothing of the fellow; besides that he is clearly an oaf and a bully and has seriously damaged a framed portrait to which I was quite attached."

"Indeed" returned Holmes, "I am sorry for that. Mind you, we are not quite as ignorant of our visitor as you imply."

"You know him then?"

"Certainly not, Watson. However, if you pass me yesterday's 'paper I may be able to give you his name."

I found the newspaper, which still lay beside my chair, and passed it to Holmes. He stood for a moment, flicking eagerly through the pages. Then, he folded the broadsheet back upon itself and rapped the paper noisily with the back of his hand.

"Ah! We have him!" cried my friend. "I should be very much mistaken if we have not just had the pleasure of a visit from Colonel Benjamin T Cheese, of Abilene, Texas. He was amongst the passengers on the Holland-America Line steamer, 'Lone Star', which docked at Southampton on Wednesday."

"How on earth can you be so sure?" I replied.

"Did you not hear him? His vocabulary and accent were sufficient to place him in Texas. A cattle-man, I'd say, judging by his dress and conversation. His readiness to resort to firearms adds to the impression I'm sure you will allow…and there was the gun itself; not the pocket piece or service revolver we're used to, but the calibre and long barrel of the Westerner. Don't you agree?"

"Granted," I replied, "but this Cheese can't be the only 'cowboy' loose in London."

"Indeed not, Watson, but our visitor has been here only a day or two at the most."

"How can you be so sure?" I asked.

"Why Watson, is it not obvious? Even the slowest-witted, or least observant of our American cousins, swiftly realise that their accustomed dress is unsuited either to our society or climate. Within a few days, every visitor from the New World, no matter how hard-bitten, has abandoned his wide brim and dusty cut-aways for a silk hat and black frock-coat."

"True" I agreed.

"Yet our visitor still wore his Texan suit and sported a six-gun in his waistband. He won't get much business done that way; and will conform to our ways soon. I'd say he has been here less than a week and when you consider that the 'Lone Star' docked on Wednesday, I feel confident in identifying our man. The other disembarking passengers were married couples, a clergyman, and two returning Britons. No, I fancy this Colonel Cheese is our man."

"But Holmes," I asked, "how on earth shall we find the fellow again? I presume you have no intention of letting this matter drop?"

"Certainly not, Watson. I hope too that you will feel sufficiently aggrieved to join me in tracking the Colonel down. I take such an order to desist as a positive injunction to do the very opposite. Besides, I feel we have a duty to find out who this Valdes is. I fear that the hot-headed Colonel may treat him with rather less restraint than he showed here."

"I am ready and willing" I replied promptly.

"Capital," responded my friend. "Then I think the best we can do is to secure an early night. We cannot begin our quest before the morning, so an early breakfast and away! Find your service revolver, Watson, and see that it is ready for action."

***

In fact, I breakfasted alone the next morning. Holmes had gone out before seven o'clock, leaving word with Mrs Hudson that I should expect his return by ten. I was brushing the last crumbs of toast from my waistcoat when my friend reappeared. He sat down heavily and gulped down half a cup of luke-warm tea.

"Ah, Watson," he gasped, "it will be another warm day. Yet warmer still I hope for Colonel Benjamin Cheese."

"You have confirmed our visitor's identity then?" I asked.

"Indeed, Watson. It was a simple enough matter. You saw me go the window last night? I watched our over-sized American depart and leap into a cab only two or three doors down Baker Street. With the number of the cab, it was easy enough (though tiring in this heat) to track down the cabby and to ascertain his destination."

Holmes drained the tea-cup before continuing his tale.

"Our boisterous visitor took a cab straight to the Kensington Hotel. I was there myself before nine this morning but even so, he had already left for Charing Cross Station. The staff of both the hotel and station easily identified Cheese from my description, and by nine-thirty I had tracked him down to the ticket office, where he bought a return ticket to Roke Common. I then hastened back to bring you up to date, my dear fellow."

"Do you intend to await Cheese's return at his hotel?"

"A sound stratagem, Watson, and an appealing one in this infernal heat. However, I am rather anxious to find the mysterious Valdes. Our best hope of doing so is through Cheese himself and I fancy we would succeed in that only if he did not suspect we were on his trail."

"What then?" I asked, standing and taking my hat from the back of the door.

"We shall take the eleven-fifteen to Roke Common. It is a tiny hamlet and I imagine we can readily pick up the trail again there."

The journey, in the baking summer heat, seemed long and uncomfortable. Our train was on a rattling, jolting suburban line, with numerous stops at simple clap-board stations and halts. Finally we arrived at Roke Common, which boasted little more than thirty or forty paces of plank platform and a cluster of small, rustic dwellings. Flies buzzed and the hot air shimmered around our train as it pulled slowly away from us.

The buildings of the hamlet were as I'd expected but instead of a single ticket collector, hugging the shade of the wooden waiting room, the dusty station yard was filled with policeman and half a dozen milling vehicles. There was a hubbub of raised voices and a scrum of what were, unmistakeably, City newspapermen, shouting questions at our old friend Inspector Lestrade.

Sherlock Holmes's pale face seemed paler still as he stared at the crowd. He fanned his face briefly with his straw hat and murmured, more to himself than to me: "A murder…it must be a murder. What else would draw the metropolitan press to Roke Common?" Before I could respond, Lestrade had seen us and beckoned us to join him.

"I'm glad to see you Mr Holmes…and Dr Watson. Not for the first time, Mr Holmes, you seem to know of a remote crime almost before we Police hear of it ourselves."

"I assure you we know nothing of whatever has happened here. We are in pursuit of a tall, angry American. A Colonel Benjamin Cheese, who has business with someone in the vicinity of Roke Common. Cheese is a giant of a man and has ill temper enough to make us concerned for this person's safety – but beyond those facts I know very little for certain."

"Well now," replied Lestrade, "that is interesting in itself. You see, an American answering your Mr Cheese's description arrived by the first train of the morning and asked for directions to 'The Red House'; which is a modest shooting box down by the river. An hour or so later, a boy employed at 'The Red House' came racing back to the station here for help, saying that murder was being done to Mr and Mrs ..." here Lestrade flicked swiftly through his notebook... " Valdes."

"That is our man," sighed Holmes. "I trust you reached them in time."

"In time to arrest the American for the murder of Mr Valdes," replied Lestrade, "that is all. He is a brute, Mr Holmes, and we can get nothing out of him. I should be grateful for anything you can tell us or deduce from him. Mrs Valdes is suffering from shock and has said nothing to clarify this sad business either. It would help us too, Dr Watson, if you would take care of her until our police surgeon arrives."

The inspector led us down a rutted carriageway through the trees to a modest house, of orange-red brick, with outbuildings forming an open courtyard before it. In the stables, we could see our visitor from the previous night, surrounded by half a dozen wary-looking constables. As we approached, a sergeant stepped forward.

"He's an animal Inspector. We've taken two pistols off him but he's still knocked Constable Jarvis here out cold with his fists and caught Thompson a cruel blow on the knee with his boot. I've taken the precaution of hand-cuffing him to the stall here but I still wouldn't go too close."

"Thank you sergeant," replied Lestrade. "Has he said anything about the dead man?"

"He's said nothing", replied the sergeant, "besides telling us a dozen times that he has 'diplomatic immunity' and that we have no right to hold him."

Lestrade cast an eye over his injured constables. "Very diplomatic" he murmured and then turned back to us. "Please come into the house gentlemen. We have our man but I cannot make head nor tail of it all. You see, this Colonel Cheese could easily have made his escape but instead he stayed in and around the house, as though he was searching for something. He has turned out all the drawers upstairs and left the box room in a state that would horrify even the most slovenly of wives or maidservants. Mrs Valdes saw it all I think, but she is in a daze to say the least and hasn't said a word. Perhaps you can tell us what happened within from the displaced furniture. I can assure you we have touched nothing."

Holmes put an arm across the threshold to prevent us entering. He then dropped to his knees and began a minute examination of the shooting box's ground floor from its carpets to its gas lamps. After ten minutes or so, Holmes stood and allowed us to enter.

"Cheese caught them off their guard," he said. "He entered by the French windows, which were ajar, and almost immediately knocked Mr Valdes to the ground. Mrs Valdes seems to have leapt up in the air then, either onto her chair (which I think unlikely) or to attack Cheese. Indeed, for a few steps, the imprint of Cheese's oversize boots in the carpet is unusually heavy, even for him. I fancy gentlemen that Mrs Valdes was clinging to Cheese's neck, spinning around with him as he fought to disengage."

"Good Heavens" remarked Lestrade, scribbling into his notebook.

"It was an unequal contest" continued Sherlock Holmes, "and ended with the unfortunate woman being flung across the room, overturning her work-basket and spilling its contents, as you see." Holmes pointed to a trail of wool, needles and thread, which lay along the wall beside a dresser.

"Poor woman" I murmured but Holmes silenced me with a gesture.

"Not so, Watson. There was more fight in Mrs Valdes than in her husband. He lay here, beside the fireplace, probably unconscious. She rose again, seizing some weapon, I suspect a knitting needle, and advanced on Cheese once more. For some reason, she dropped it again beside her overturned chair…here."

"Perhaps Cheese drew his revolver?" I suggested.

"Very possibly, Watson," nodded my friend, "I fancy this brute would not be above threatening to shoot her husband as he lay senseless, if it secured his control over Mrs Valdes. At any rate something did, for she set aside her weapon and sat there in the wicker chair, while Cheese paced to and fro. He smoked a thin American cigar, probably a cheroot, as he paced; scattering ash as he went but considerate enough to throw its butt through the French window when he had finished."

"You saw the cigar as we arrived?" asked Lestrade.

"No, but it is not in the room and I cannot think that even Cheese would toss it away through the door to the hall."

"Quite so" nodded Lestrade, still scribbling.

"Perhaps I should attend to Mrs Valdes?" I suggested and Lestrade led us into the kitchen of the house, where two local policeman stood beside the unfortunate woman. Mrs Valdes sat in a motionless rocking chair. She was deathly pale, despite an olive complexion, and stared blankly ahead through dark, Spanish eyes.

I knelt beside her to examine her. "It is a case of shock" I said. "As severe as any I've seen; even as an Army surgeon on India's North-West Frontier. Keep her warm, perhaps with a dose of brandy, and I think she'll recover soon. At least enough to tell us something of what has happened here."

I was mistaken however. Mrs Valdes was eventually conveyed to the local cottage hospital, where she recovered physically but not mentally. Cheese himself never stood trial. To our utter disgust, his claim of diplomatic immunity proved to have some truth to it. The charge was first reduced from murder to manslaughter, with some suggestion that Mr Valdes had launched a murderous assault upon Cheese, and then dropped altogether. The violent-tempered Colonel was escorted, protesting every inch of the way, to the next boat for Galveston and expelled from the country.

I had imagined that Holmes would leave the matter there but to my surprise he seemed obsessed with the case. Having brooded and fretted over it for some days, he finally suggested another visit to Mrs Valdes. The poor woman seemed no better and raved throughout our brief visit about Cheese, her husband's innocence and her 'bonds'. It was a pitiful scene, to see what must once have been a Spanish or Mexican beauty, rubbing at her wrists and bemoaning the constriction of her binding.

"But Watson," remarked Sherlock Holmes, as we travelled back to Charing Cross, "there was no suggestion or sign that Cheese had bound Mrs Valdes's wrists."

"Yes," I agreed, "perhaps she was remembering a previous occasion. I have a distinct impression that the Valdeses had fled from the United States to escape Cheese, or his associates."

Holmes nodded slowly, tapping a fresh cigarette pensively on his thumb nail. "You are certainly correct that Cheese was in pursuit of Valdes and his wife. I am certain too that last week's was not his first visit to Roke Common. I rather fancy, Watson, that Cheese went down into Kent immediately after arriving in London. He thought to intimidate the Valdeses and they threatened him in return with the one name they had heard linked to British justice – Sherlock Holmes!"

"Of course" I replied. "They told Cheese that you were retained to protect them, thinking that he would leave them alone. Instead, he stormed straight to Baker Street to warn us off the case. Yet what was it that made Cheese so determined to seek out and persecute so innocent a couple?"

"Precisely Watson," replied Holmes, "though I am bound to point out that we have no evidence of Mr Valdes's innocence, even if we consider him ultimately ill-used by Cheese. Indeed, did not the Colonel describe him as 'that thief Valdes' on the occasion of his visit to us?"

I was about to reply, when my friend was suddenly convulsed in a paroxysm of anger or frustration. He slapped at his forehead and raged: "Ah! Watson, what a fool I have been. The whole case was before us all the time! Literally before us!"

"But Holmes," I expostulated, "I cannot see…"

"Come Watson," interrupted my friend, leaping to his feet as we slowly pulled into a sleepy station, "we must return to Roke Common. Oh, how blind I have been."

We hurried from our train and, by sheer good fortune into another, waiting at the adjacent platform, bound for stations including Roke Common. It was another twenty-five minutes before we reached the drive to the Valdes's shooting box, yet Sherlock Holmes said not another word beyond occasional mutterings at his own folly, blindness, or the need for haste. A further ten minutes elapsed before we stood, together with the local policeman, in the Valdes's hallway.

Holmes paused for a moment, like a hound sniffing out a scent, and then strode swiftly through each room of the house. He thrust his head through each doorway, looking this way and that, moving on with a gasp of frustration. At length only the attic bedrooms remained. Each in turn proved unsatisfactory, until we reached a long, low servants' room; empty of furniture, yet newly swept and decorated with distinctive, green striped paper.

Holmes gave a snort of satisfaction and leapt at the wall, scrabbling at the wallpaper. The constable and I watched in astonishment, as two or three sections of the paper, each perhaps a foot long by eight or nine inches, came away complete in his hands. Sherlock Holmes almost danced for joy, laughing and crying out.

"The bonds, Watson. The *bonds*! These are what Mrs Valdes raved about. They weren't handcuffs or ropes used on the Valdeses by Cheese; they were the Texan State government bonds stolen perhaps from the Colonel by his Mexican servants. The front is highly decorated, bearing the single star and other symbols or badges of Texas, while the reverse is just lined in green. Ha! What a way to conceal loot, eh, Watson? Simply paste it onto the wall!"

On our long, hot, journey home, Holmes advanced a theory which enquiries subsequently proved to be largely correct. The Valdes family was employed on Colonel Cheese's Texan ranch and in the running of his business interests. They had, apparently, defrauded their employer and fled to Europe and then London to make good their escape.

Holmes declined to speculate further but I still maintain that had Cheese so clear a case against his servants, he need simply have informed the authorities here to obtain redress. I am convinced that so violent a murderer (for so I regard him) as Cheese must have positively driven the Valdeses to crime. No other reason could possibly have caused so beautiful a woman and her weak, yet honest husband, to take such a desperate a step against him.

"Cheese had only himself to blame," I declared after a few minutes' thought, but Holmes had already placed his hat over his eyes and surrendered to sleep and the gentle motion of the train.

The Adventure of the Spurned Lover

To my friend Sherlock Holmes the solution of a case was generally its own reward. Once solved, it ceased to occupy his thoughts. Justice was meted out and the case could be safely consigned to the scrapbook. My chronicles were merely exemplars of his deductive methods, to be drawn upon as object lessons or instances for future comparison.

Clients, too, were rarely referred to again, though occasionally we would learn of their doings by letter or newspaper report. There were also chance meetings in the street. On only one occasion, do I recall my friend actually seeking out a past enquirer and then, having done so, to my utter surprise, he sought out another!

It was a dismal day in London, damp and cold, and I was glad to reach the warmth of our old rooms in Baker Street. My spirits rose further with the effusion of Sherlock Holmes's greeting.

"Ah, Watson, how timely. I am expecting a visitor shortly and I would beg you to remain and act once again as my assistant and chronicler."

"Certainly" I replied, "whom are we expecting?"

My friend threw back his head and laughed. "Truly one of the most unsavoury of fellows, Watson. You will scarcely approve but I insist that you stay."

Holmes selected a pipe from the mantle-piece and said not another word until its tobacco was glowing red-hot and he was settled comfortably in a fire-side chair.

"Our visitor's name is Potiphar Silk, Watson. I knew him first as one of the official detective police. He was a promising officer but a tendency to drink on duty and an over eagerness (alas) to secure a conviction or two, which were not quite merited by the evidence, led to his dismissal from the Force."

I frowned and clicked my tongue.

"There is worse yet, Watson. Poor Potiphar now makes a reasonable living from divorce cases and other distasteful domestic legal business. Many a noble marriage has foundered upon Potiphar's evidence and I am aware of two breach of promise cases and a disinheritance at the highest levels of society, which were brought to profitable conclusions thanks to his efforts."

"Profitable conclusions?" I replied, "I wonder that you'll let the fellow across your threshold Holmes".

"Potiphar Silk may not be my companion of choice, Watson, but he has been decidedly useful in the past and, if his trade is vile, he does nevertheless operate according to a code of honour, strange and twisted though it may be. Besides, surely only those who behave improperly need fear a scandal."

"Pah!" I retorted. "You know these fellows have neither scruples nor mercy."

I may have said more but I fell silent at the sound of a visitor at the street door and shortly after, Mr Potiphar Silk was admitted. There was still much of the policeman in his appearance and manner; a squat fellow in a short coat and curly-brimmed bowler hat. He was business-like too and wasted no time in getting to the matter in hand. He sat forward in his chair, a cigar in one hand and a glass of whisky in the other.

Silk's voice, when at last he spoke more than to grunt in gratitude for his chair, cigar and drink, surprised me for its smooth, lilting quality. I guessed that Silk's origins lay not in London but somewhere on the Marches of Wales.

"Thank you for seeing me again Mr Holmes. I am not overly proud of my business (though it is an honest enough living) and many doors remain firmly shut in my face. I confess this time though I have stumbled on something quite out of my line. Let me explain gentlemen. I know you're busy men and I assure you I shall not say an unnecessary word."

Holmes smiled to himself at this and sat back in his chair, his fingers raised before him in an arch.

"Well, gentlemen, I am currently engaged in a divorce case. I'll not mention the parties. I needn't and even I have some discretion, but suffice it to say that a noble husband's neglect has led to a noble wife's disloyalty. It is sad, very sad."

The hypocrisy of the rogue appalled me but I remained silent out of respect for Holmes. Instead I took a swig of my own drink. Silk turned a baleful eye upon me.

"I know what you are thinking Dr Watson. Ten years ago, with a career in the police ahead of me, I would have agreed. Needs must however and a man is a fool who does not make use of what few talents he possesses."

Silk accepted another tot of whisky and continued his tale.

"For a month and a half I have pursued that noble lady. There is little doubt in the case. However, in the last week two things changed. First, the man in the case suddenly left a perfectly good house, rented for the season as far I can tell, and moved into the Royal Piccadilly Hotel. Then the 'affair' itself seemed off. I thought at first that my lady's husband had won back her affections. Candidly, gentlemen, he has not. He is too stupid to see what he is losing and too proud to try in any case. No, gentlemen, it is the ardour of the 'other' man in her life which has cooled – cooled suddenly and cooled almost to ice."

"How does this affect us?" asked Sherlock Holmes, his eyes now closed and a thin coil of smoke rising from the bowl of his long stemmed pipe.

"Well", responded our visitor, "if I were to use the phrase 'he's a different man' I would do so meaning it literally, rather than metaphorically."

Holmes's eyes opened. "Does the lady not know her lover?"

"That's just it gentlemen. She remains ardent despite his constant repulsion. The fact is, I wouldn't know myself but for my little habit of photography. You see, gentlemen, I like to have a photograph of those I'm employed to watch. It ensures, at the beginning of a case, that I'm following the right lady or man. Usually, a client will provide me with a *carte-de-visite* of his or her spouse and I'll take my own of the other 'subject' as we call them. Sometimes, I take or obtain several, to hand out to my colleagues, do you see?"

Holmes nodded, while I slowly shook my head – in disbelief rather than incomprehension. Silk examined his cigar thoughtfully before proceeding, his voice somewhat quieter and more eager.

"well, in this case my client had given me two photographs; one of his wife and the other of her supposed lover. He's a public figure, a Member of Parliament. It was only this morning when I chanced to look carefully at the two photographs I had of the 'lover', that I realised something had changed". Silk paused for a moment and then carefully withdrew two *carte-de-visite* photographs from an inner pocket. One, I could see, was pasted onto cheap, plain card. The other was on the cream pasteboard with the arms and advertising of a court photographer.

"See for yourself" said Silk, handing the photographs across to Holmes. For a moment my friend hesitated. Then he stood and carried them across to our brightest lamp, where he examined both images with the aid of his lens. Finally, he passed them to me.

I confess I could see no difference. One, from the court studio, showed an elegant man in morning dress, leaning upon a pillar, on which he had placed his silk hat.

The other showed the same man, similarly dressed, though wearing his hat, seemingly in conversation with an unseen person.

"I should explain" interrupted Silk, "that it takes some skill to get so clear an image. Usually, we can hide our camera and then detain the 'subject' of our portrait with an inconsequential question or two while we snap our shutter so to speak. It is quite an art and occasionally has clinched a case…"

I snorted, horrified at the lengths to which such skills might be put. "Well," I declared, "I see no difference, unless wearing rather than carrying a hat constitutes a shocking alteration of character".

"Really Watson", responded Sherlock Holmes. "Try a little harder and use my lens."

I studied the portraits. Nothing seemed out of place. Seemingly they were photographs of the same man. Then, at the point of giving up, I focussed the lens upon the right hands of both men. One wore a ring, a gold signet ring I would have said, but the other did not.

"There is a ring missing?" I ventured. "A ring can be lost or simply discarded."

Holmes smiled encouragement and gestured towards the photographs again. "Look again at the faces, Watson. Look at the left cheek."

I did so and saw immediately that while one face had a prominent mole an inch or so below the ear, the other did not.

"An unsightly mole? Why a clever photographer could easily remove that!"

Silk's voice responded this time: "Very true Dr Watson. But the mole is there on the court photographer's image. It is *my* photograph which lacks it!"

I returned to the photographs, my heart beginning to race as the possibilities of this mystery began to fill my mind. This time my eye was 'in' and I saw what had excited our visitor.

"The jaw is different. It is slight but there is a definite difference in shape. The nose too and even the eyebrows…or is it the shape of the brows? Why, this *is* a different man…but a deuced cunning imposture!"

Silk set down his whisky glass and tossed the butt of his cigar into our fire. His business was clearly all but done.

"Well now gentlemen, you have the puzzle. My case is now irresolvable until the lady errs again (as she will) but yours is before you. The man is Sir Archibald Freke; a Member of Parliament…or, at least, he *was* until someone else took to personation of him. I cannot go to the police; my history precludes that I fear. So, I came to you Mr Holmes and I go now happy to leave the case in your hands. Pick it up or leave it as you will. I fancy we shall hear more of it before too long in any case."

Holmes sat in silence for more than an hour. Then, just as my thoughts were beginning to shift from the mystery of Sir Archibald Freke, M.P., towards the surer ground of dinner, my friend leapt from his chair and seized his hat.

"Come Watson, let us return the compliment of an erstwhile client and pay a visit upon Mr Trelawney Hope. The newspaper tells me Parliament is sitting, so we shall seek him at Westminster rather than at home."

"But Holmes," I objected, "this business of Freke may be nothing more than a domestic scandal. Have we the right to open it up to the scrutiny of his parliamentary colleagues?"

Holmes paused in the doorway, his finger thoughtfully at his lips. For a moment he seemed distracted but snapped suddenly back into his decisive self.

"No Watson, we have plunged into dark waters. There is more here than a sordid *affaire de coeur* and I fear we need the aid of a sure footed politician. Trelawney Hope has proved his discretion and we cannot doubt his knowledge of Parliament. We must find a cab, as I fear there is little time to lose."

***

Mr Trelawney Hope had changed greatly in the two years or so since we had last seen him in the affair of the 'Second Stain'. Neither Holmes nor I were close followers of politics but we were aware that he had lost his place as European Secretary following the election and now acted as Chief Whip for his party.

It was no sinecure. They were still in government, yet with so strong an Irish Home Rule faction in the House, Lord Bellinger remained Prime Minister almost at the whim of the Irish votes. Were the Home Rulers to switch to the opposition, Bellinger's majority would be cut to a single vote.

Mr Trelawney Hope's first words confirmed as much. "We limp on, Mr Holmes. We dare not attempt any great measure of reform simply because it would seal our fate…and a resort to the country would be catastrophic. Lord Bellinger hopes for the best but I fear we are doomed to a lengthy period of opposition when the 'crash' comes – as come it must."

Trelawney Hope's demeanour mirrored his prognostications. I was shocked to see how, in a matter of ten or a dozen short months, fate had dealt so cruelly with him. His once bright eyes were dimmed and his trim figure had turned to fat, adding jowls to his jaw-line and bulging creases to his once trim waistcoat.

"You are estranged from Lady Hilda, I see" remarked Sherlock Holmes "and you have taken to dining, if not actually *living* at your club. Trust…trust, Mr Trelawney Hope is such a vital ingredient I marriage, is it not?"

I was astonished at Holmes's candour, yet the politician merely shrugged his shoulders.

"Indeed, Mr Holmes. No wife would see her husband so shabbily turned out and you detect perhaps the chops and gravy of the club on my waistcoat? It is true, that affair of the letter did for us. I know you will not say so but I am still certain there was more to it than met the eye!"

"Nothing, I believe," replied my friend, "to merit reproach on either party, save perhaps for folly – and that in fair and equal measure. However, we trespass upon your time and have not called upon you out of a desire to meddle."

"What then?" responded the Chief Whip, sitting up in his chair and eyeing us with more suspicion.

"We seek your advice. Neither Watson nor I qualify as political *cognoscenti* yet would have a question answered. Forgive us its apparent eccentricity. What effect would the unexpected absence of a government M.P. have upon the balance of the parties?"

Trelawney Hope smiled and relaxed back into his chair. "None, gentlemen." He paused for thought and sat forward again. "One government vote less, even with the Irish against us, would still give us the bill. We might have a 'sticky' time of it but we can call upon the Speaker's vote in the case of a tie and carry the measure. We would even win a vote of confidence, though without much moral authority."

Holmes, for once, was clearly surprised. He stood, still silent and I realised that our interview was at an end. I thanked Trelawney Hope and I too stood, waiting for Holmes to turn to the door. Instead, he raised a finger, which he wagged meditatively towards our host. Quietly, almost hesitatingly he asked: "But what if the MP, rather than absent himself, voted not with you but for the Opposition?"

The Chief Whip almost blanched. "Such an act of treachery is almost unheard of. Why, it would mean not only that we were a vote down but that they were also one up. Mr Holmes, it would bring down the government!"

***

We were seated in our cab once more, hastening back to Baker Street, before Holmes spoke again. Once again I could scarcely believe my ears when he suddenly reached up with his stick to attract the attention of our driver and called out the address of the banker, Alexander Holder, for whom Holmes had once retrieved the Beryl Coronet.

"You astonish me, Holmes," I remarked. "Two ex-clients in one evening? If you seek advice again, it can only be upon financial affairs, and you have obviously then seen more in this substitution of an M.P. than I have. Is it an attempt to bring down the government? Isn't a simple practical joke a more likely explanation? Or some subterfuge to fool pursuers in a case of divorce?"

"The latter solution was my first thought Watson" replied Sherlock Holmes, "but it won't do. If this Archibald Freke is in love, why should he suddenly set up a 'double' who turns away the loved-one? If he is now 'out' of love, why not simply spurn the woman outright? No, Watson, there is a deeper plot here."

"Then is it to bring down the government?" I asked.
"I cannot see it, Watson. To pass oneself off as an M.P. might be carried out once by a daring man. In the darkness of the voting lobby, especially if he were alongside his 'enemies' instead of his friends, the 'actor' might carry it off, but to vote down an administration would inevitably draw down such limelight and observation that no greasepaint and false hair would stand the test. Exposure would be inevitable and the responsible faction would pay for one day's victory with decades of political oblivion!"

"Then what motive can there be?"

"That is a matter I wish to put to Mr Alexander Holder, Watson. We need financial knowledge now just as we needed political advice before. Ah, I see we are here. Come, Watson, we are closing in upon our prey but still we must make haste."

***

Mr Holder broke free from a dinner party to see us briefly in his hall. It was not a happy meeting on either side. I fear that it will be many more years before memories of the Beryl Coronet cease to have a baleful effect upon the banker. Neverthless, he answered Holmes's questions fully and as best he could.

Finally, he acceded to my friend's request that he telephone Inspector Lestrade, at Scotland Yard, requesting that we rendezvous at the Royal Hotel, Piccadilly. Within ten minutes Holmes and I were in our cab again, clattering the five or so miles back from Streatham to Piccadilly.

"We were wrong Watson, to seek a political motive behind this affair. If I am right, this is the work of a cartel; a gang of the wealthiest investors, eager to reap even richer rewards from their speculations."

"I see Sir Archibald Freke as their pawn in a greater game. He is an uninspiring back-bencher Watson, a loyal member of his party, whose vote can always be counted upon. There lies the simple cruelty of their plan, Watson."

"This is not a scheme to bring down the government. Far from it. Let us suppose, Watson, that one evening in Parliament, our poor, duped Sir Archibald wanders into the wrong lobby and by switching his vote, defeats a government bill. Let us say it is a measure of little importance – the Plymouth Fisheries Bill or Stoke on Trent Light Railway and Tramways Amendment – it matters not what. The Government is defeated. What will happen next?

Will there be a vote of no confidence? How will Freke vote next? What if the annual army or navy vote is defeated?"

"Think of the uncertainty, Watson. What if Freke cannot be found and no satisfactory explanation is forthcoming? What will he do next? What are his motives? Think of the uncertainty in the stock-market. Think of the fall in share prices. Remember what Holder told us of the current uncertainty in the City of London. Why, Watson, that would be the time to buy up stocks and shares as they tumbled and the City trembled."

"Then think of the relief, Watson, when Freke was found dead. The suicide of the poor fool whose blundering had caused such catastrophic losses. Didn't Holder tell us the share prices would have recovered, even risen, by the time the morning papers carried the news. The Government would be safe and capital might continue its quiet business. But our cartel, Watson, simply by buying stocks cheap and selling them again later at the top of the market, would be millions the richer for its night's work! All at the cost of a single, unregarded M.P. Why, it is as ingenious as it is evil, Watson."

We reached the Hotel just after midnight. Lestrade awaited us in the lobby. Ten minutes sufficed to tell him all we knew, or suspected. Together we approached the receptionist, a young, sleepy-looking clerk, who rose to greet us.

"Yes gentlemen?" he asked, rubbing his eyes.

"Wake up laddy" demanded Lestrade, his voice icy with menace, "Is Sir Archibald Freke in the Hotel?"

The clerk nodded vigorously, his jaw drooping with shock.

"What room? I am a policeman and I will brook no nonsense, sonny. Give me your spare key and be quick about it."

"R-r-r-room twenty-eight" stuttered the youth. "It is a suite on the first floor. Shall I find the duty manager?"

"You'll do no such thing" replied Lestrade. "Here, point out the way."

"Wait," interrupted Holmes, "Let us keep our voices low. There is nothing to be gained by advertising our presence too early. Tell me, my boy, has Mr Freke been eating well lately?"

"Eating well?" replied the clerk, incredulously.

"Has he ordered extra food? Or meals at unusual times?"

"Well, sir, he does often send down for sandwiches and beer, or a pork pie and the odd bottle of hock. Some of the porters have made fun of it rather, but…"

"Capital! We may well find both Sir Archibalds in residence. I had hoped as much."

We dashed up the main staircase, meeting only another drooping porter, carrying a tray of dirty plates and an empty beer bottle.

"Here you, is that from twenty-eight?" demanded Lestrade.

"It is" replied the porter with a yawn, "that bloke could eat fer two, I'm tellin' you. All day and all night…chomp, chomp and forever ringin' his bloomin' bell."

"That's enough," declared Lestrade, "Come on!"

We reached the door of the suite, to find it ajar. Without a word, Holmes turned upon his heels and dashed back down the staircase. I continued into the room with Lestrade, where we cried as one "Gas!" We plunged deeper into the room, our handkerchiefs held tight to our noses. A search of the dressing room revealed nothing, but in the rear bedroom we found the dishevelled figure of Sir Archibald Freke, clad in nightshirt and dressing gown, unconscious upon the bed. The gas jets were turned on full and must soon have extinguished his life, either by suffocation or explosion. We were throwing open every window, when Holmes rejoined us.

"Sir Archibald will live" I reassured him. "I can find no clue though, as to the villain behind this."

"The villain?" asked Holmes, "why it was the villain we met on the stairs! He must have heard us coming, thanks to Lestrade's bellowing, and seized that tray of crockery to make his escape."

"The porter?" I gasped.

"Of course" Holmes replied, "I'm only ashamed it took me so long to realise it. To a master of disguise, who can live a week undetected as Sir Archibald Freke, two minutes as a porter is nothing."

Lestrade sank onto the bed with a groan.

"They'll not get away with it" I cried. "Surely justice will be done?"

"I doubt it Watson. Without a parliamentary vote, not a single share will have fallen in price and none will have changed hands. Only the kidnapper has committed a crime, beyond intention at least, and we shall be hard put to trace him."

Holmes paused briefly to examine the room and the still sleeping victim of the audacious plot.

"Holmes," I asked, "why did they risk keeping Freke alive – if they meant to kill him anyway?"

"To fit their plan, Watson. Freke would have to kill himself when he discovered his 'mistake' in voting in the wrong lobby. A suicide is easily faked; a fresh corpse is not. Similarly, he moved into an unfamiliar hotel for the very reason that it *is* unfamiliar. There would be no servants or friends of the real Sir Archibald Freke to notice the deception."

"They must not escape!" I declared.

"Perhaps when Sir Archibald awakes he may have a clue for Lestrade. It is a matter for Scotland Yard now. I have no doubt, Watson, that in any case, they'll try again sooner rather than later. This is far too good a scheme to abandon because of a grain or two of ill luck. No, we shall hear of these scoundrels again and we shall have them then, rest assured."

The Augean Stables

The wagonette we had hired from Coombe Tracey jolted up the rutted track from the town onto Dartmoor. I sat beside Holmes in the back, while Lestrade (to keep the best balance) sat opposite us, behind the driver. The climax of our case against Stapleton in the affair of the Baskerville Hound was rapidly approaching and our excitement was palpable. Lestrade and I both leaned towards Holmes, eager to continue our planning, but Holmes cocked an eye towards our driver and shook his head in warning.

As we creaked and lurched ever deeper onto the Moor, the damp air settled into our bones and we nestled into our overcoats, thrusting our hands deep into our pockets. Lestrade seemed lulled into sleep by the swaying of our conveyance but I could not relax. At length Sherlock Holmes, perhaps sensing my tenseness, leaned closer to me and spoke, in a low voice, close to my ear.

"You know, Watson, there was a time when I imagined detective work could be done almost entirely in the abstract, with scarcely any need to venture from what I saw as my 'consulting' room. Indeed, I styled myself a 'consulting detective'; a clearing house, you might say, for information and advice."

"But you would have missed the charm of the outdoors," I joked, with a nod towards the forbidding damp and grey landscape that surrounded us.

"Indeed I would, Watson," nodded my friend with a wry smile. "Nevertheless, it was as a purely consulting detective that I began my career. You will remember the succession of clients in those early days, and how often you were expelled from your own sitting room. Ah, Watson, they were dreary days indeed; of lost dogs, misplaced jewellery, and trifling decisions to be made between rivals for love or applicants for a position."

"Yet it is remarkable what can be done without leaving Baker Street, simply from a consideration of the facts," I suggested.

Sherlock Holmes laughed quietly to himself.

"Hardly, Watson," he said, "though there was one case…"

"Really?" I asked, sliding closer to my friend and urging him to tell me more.

"Well, I suppose it would beguile away the hour or so we have before us, until we reach Merripit House. Tell me, my dear Watson, have your afternoon strolls ever taken you as far as the Dalrymple Gallery?"

"Off Portman Square?" I asked, "yes, I know it."

"You have seen their Rubens? The great "Cleansing of the Augean Stables?"

"A massive work," I replied, "something of a daub, I always think but striking for its size if nothing else."

Holmes nodded again. "I rather agree, Watson. Hardly Rubens's subtlest painting but a curious subject and, I believe, notably as his largest work. That, coupled to an exciting history with several of the world's most bloodthirsty tyrants as former owners, has made 'the Cleansing' one of the art world's most sought after paintings."

"You will readily imagine my interest," continued Sherlock Holmes, "when I learned that it had been stolen."

"But it would take an army of thieves and the largest waggon in London just to remove the painting!" I ejaculated.

"Quite so. You merely repeat what I said myself," replied Holmes. "I recall that you were away for the weekend and I was therefore excused the necessity of begging the sole use of our sitting room for yet another consultation. My client was Lord Robert Bolton, a tall, elegant fellow of perhaps forty years of age, dressed in the height of fashion. He was clearly ill at ease throughout our interview and directed his gaze at first as though he were addressing an imaginary figure seated some way to my right.

" "It would be best, my lord," said I, "if you were to tell me everything. From the beginning. Please give me every detail and omit nothing, however trivial or inconsequential it may seem."

Holmes pulled his travelling rug closer about him. A slight smile stole across his lips, as he remembered his meeting with the director of the Dalrymple Gallery.

"It seems, Watson, that the thieves (ten or eleven in number) had entered the gallery an hour before it was due to open to the public. They wore uniforms similar to those of the regular attendants and behaved entirely as though they were on legitimate business. They marched straight to the Rubens, which had been lowered from its usual position on the wall, while some repair to the new electric lighting was done, and carried it out of the gallery as though it were the most natural action in the world!"

"I recollect that my amusement annoyed Lord Robert. Now the Rubens, Watson, is actually painted on wood – rather than canvas – and is held together with a considerable framework of struts and spars. Nevertheless, the painting was lifted up and carried out of the gallery, through its front door."

"Did no-one attempt to stop them?" I asked.

"Indeed they did, Watson. The deputy director of the gallery, no less, actually arrived for work, just as the Rubens was leaving. The poor fellow was quietly overpowered and left bound and gagged behind the cloakroom counter. One attendant also attempted to intervene and he was also found by the police amongst the cloaks, having been knocked unconscious."

"Astonishing" I murmured.

"Oh, yes, Watson, quite the simplest yet most audacious theft in years." Holmes cocked an eye towards the dozing Lestrade and continued his tale in an even lower tone: "The police, needless to say, were utterly baffled. They were energetic, it is true, but ineffectual. Despite their best endeavours they picked up not a single thread. I well recall the utter frustration of Lord Robert Bolton. He leapt from our best chair Watson and actually stamped upon the floor in his wrath."

" "The largest piece of Flemish art in London – if not Europe – and it vanishes into thin air! How can it?" he cried, "how can it? Policemen everywhere, yet not a soul can be found who saw either their vehicle or a veritable army of uniformed attendants wandering about Portman Square with it in their arms! It is an outrage, Holmes! An outrage and a catastrophe!" "

"Now, as you well know my dear Watson," purred Holmes, "there is always *someone* in London to see events unfold. I fancy there is not a minute of the day and not an inch of our city's streets which is not observed by someone. Yet the Metropolitan Police found not a single witness to this most obvious of crimes."

Holmes was momentarily distracted by our driver but soon returned to his story. "I had just managed to coax Lord Robert back into our chair, Watson, when there came a desperate ringing at the front door and an attendant from the gallery was admitted with an urgent message for its director. The poor fellow stood in our doorway, mopping his brow and gasping for breath, as he had run all the way from Portman Square. He handed over a long, cream coloured envelope, which Lord Robert tore open."

"We both watched aghast, as the director of the Dalrymple Gallery swiftly scanned the contents of the letter and then, with a cry, collapsed backwards in a faint."

"You will be pleased to hear that I dosed the poor fellow with brandy, Watson, before sitting him up with a loosened collar, while I examined the message which had proved so devastating."

"The whole was a model of brevity and therefore of little use to the *consulting* detective. The envelope was of the type sold in their thousands every day by stationers throughout London. It was addressed in a somewhat powdery, well-watered blue-black ink, of which gallons must be mixed every week in a thousand banks, hotels and post offices. The nib confirmed my diagnosis, Watson. It was well worn and had 'sputtered' in no fewer than six places."

"What did the letter say?" I asked.

"Oh, rather what you might have expected," replied Holmes, almost wearily, "it was directed to 'Lord Robert Bolton' and marked 'MOST URGENT' with two under-linings."

"The letter itself was no more helpful to me. It was in the same ink and had been written in a disguised hand."

"A disguised hand?" I queried.

"Yes, Watson, I should say that it had been written by a right-handed man, using his left hand. It was a passable, if somewhat scrawled copper-plate."

"Were there any features of interest?"

"Oh yes, Watson, the paper itself was quite curious and despite the attempts to conceal the fact, it was still a distinctive hand. The capitals were elaborately formed and both the ascending and descending loops were unusually elongated. I have no doubt that the writing alone would have convicted the thief had we laid our hands upon him; but of course we had not. Moreover, Lord Robert was insistent that he did not recognise the writing."

"How was the paper curious?" I asked.

Holmes threw back his head and laughed, though he was careful to choke back his customary bark, so as not to wake our sleeping comrade. "The message was written on the back of a handbill advertising firewood. A cruel irony, considering the message itself."

"What was the message?"

"It simply stated that unless a carpet bag, containing one thousand pounds, was hung on the railings outside the Gallery at nine that evening, then the Rubens would join the kindling offered for sale 'overleaf'."

"But how on earth could they hope to get away with such a crime? Surely even the police could arrest whoever collected the money, or at least follow them to the lair of the villain behind the theft, if he were an innocent agent?"

"Indeed, Watson, but think of the risks. I fancy I, or you, could elude any but the most determined and fortunate pursuer. Think of the tricks to be played with cabs, or the underground railway. No, Watson, with the Rubens at stake, it would be a bold man indeed, who would venture all on a premature springing of the trap."

"But how else could the painting be recovered? Was Lord Robert prepared to pay such a sum? Could the Dalrymple Gallery find it at such short notice?" I turned in my seat to find Holmes smiling to himself at the memory of the crisis.

"I began," continued Holmes, "to question my two visitors about the Gallery and its *environs*. I had a pretty good knowledge of the district, even then, but they told me much more. Gradually, I began to see the Square in my mind's eye, from the cab stand at the Gloucester Place end to the new offices of the Capital and Counties Bank rising slowly behind their hoardings on the corner of Orchard Street. I began to circle above it, like a bird of prey, Watson, considering every aspect and angle of the gallery and surrounding area. I questioned both Lord Robert and the attendant closely. Where one's memory or knowledge failed, the other spoke up.

I fancy that after an hour or so's questioning, I could have drawn a map of the area to equal the largest scale offered by the Ordnance Survey; but I knew so much more. I had the smells, the litter, and the traffic (both human and otherwise). I knew the cries of the street vendors and I could have told you almost every sale or musical hall act with a bill or advertisement pasted across the Capital and Counties building site."

Holmes's lips twitched with pleasure.

"I might add, Watson, that I also had the solution to the case!"

"You had solved the case?" I ejaculated. "You could recover the painting?"

"Indeed, Watson. Without straying further than our sideboard for a decanter of brandy."

"But how was it done?" I asked in astonishment. "How had they spirited away so massive a painting and how can you possibly have determined its hiding place.?"

Holmes rearranged his travelling rug about his knees and craned his long neck around the bulk of our driver, to ascertain our progress towards Merripit House. Lestrade slumbered on. Holmes turned back to me, his eyes twinkling with merriment.

"Well, Watson, I believe the solution of the case lay in an assessment of the criminals with whom we were dealing."

"Utter rogues, I would say," I answered, "playing with one of the most famous paintings of the seventeenth century, as though it were firewood!"

Holmes slapped his knees and uttered a cry of delight. "Ah, Watson! How often do you see through the mists and fogs of a case. Truly, your mind is like a beam from one of the new carbide lamps."

"Really?" I asked, incredulity mingling with pleasure.

"Of course," replied my friend with a chuckle, "if only you could see your own skill for what is!"

"I must confess I am in some confusion still" I replied.

"Well," responded Holmes, "you have just stated the key to the solution of this puzzle. Lord Robert Bolton was a victim of rogues, *playing* with an Old Master."

Holmes's hands emerged from beneath his travelling rug, his long fingers counting off the points as he made them: "The means of the theft itself was audacious, one might almost say 'impertinent', or even 'insolent;' simply walking in and taking the painting from under the noses of its custodians. The choice of painting – the largest in the gallery – shows some panache, you'll agree, and the selection of a handbill for firewood, when any scrap of paper would have sufficed, suggests a certain degree of humour, does it not?"

"It hardly seems a matter for humour to me," I retorted.

"Oh, come, come Watson. This is a prank. Even the ransom demanded, a mere thousand pounds when ten times that sum could have been raised by the Gallery and its supporters, speaks more to me of a practical joke than the deepest, darkest villainy."

I smiled and confessed that there was something in what Holmes had to say. "But Holmes," I added, "how did you solve the case?"

"Remember, Watson, the keys to this puzzle are before you. The painting was carried by a dozen 'attendants' from the Gallery. It reached the Square, yet not a soul saw it leave; either on their shoulders or in any sort of vehicle."

"It was still in the Square then!"

"Exactly, Watson. But where?"

I wracked my brains. "The cab stand is too small. Could it be the bank?" I asked.

"Ah, Watson" replied my friend. "But the police had searched the bank. It was the ideal place perhaps. Shielded from view by wooden hoardings, temporarily deserted at the weekend and with half built underground strong-rooms, yet on Monday it would swarm with labourers - all of them agog to see Rubens's largest (if not finest) work abandoned in their midst. No, Watson, guess again!"

"There is nowhere else" I cried.

"Think of Mr Poe's purloined letter, Watson. Where best to hide a stolen paper than amongst other papers? Hide a book in a library, Watson. Slip a knife into a knife drawer if you would see it overlooked!"

"They carried the painting back into the Gallery?" I asked incredulously. "Surely, someone would notice that Rubens. Why, it is the size of two farm gates!"

"Ha! Watson! You are the audacious one here!" cried Holmes, throwing his head back in a guffaw, which woke Lestrade and caused our driver to pull on his reins and halt the waggonette.

"Yes, driver" called Holmes, throwing off his travelling rug, "this will do very well. Merripit House is but a short walk up this avenue of trees. We shall do better to approach from here on foot. Come, Lestrade, look to your weapon and your lamp. You are armed Lestrade?"

I climbed down beside Holmes, eager to hear the last of one adventure before we embarked upon another.

"Holmes," I whispered, "where was the painting? Was it recovered?"

"Why yes, Watson. Those desperadoes of yours had indeed carried it to the Bank but they had then reversed it and nailed it up as part of the hoarding around the building site. A few posters and handbills pasted across the back of the painting and it served very well to keep out idlers and naughty children!"

"But who had stolen it?"

"Ah, Watson, that I cannot say. I had returned the Augean Stables to the Dalrymple Collection and pocketed a fee of twenty five guineas. I had no desire to interfere with the police investigation and certainly nothing to gain by seeing a dozen jokers confined in one of Her Majesty's gaols."

"A dozen jokers?" I stammered.

"Quite so, Watson. Let us say 'a *team* of them, with one reserve'. Now, gentlemen, that is Merripit House and the end of our journey. I must request you to walk on tiptoe and not to talk above a whisper."

The Affair of the involuntary Spy

My friend Sherlock Holmes was never entirely at ease with women. Almost invariably they were a complicating factor in his cases. He would rail against their reliance upon feelings as opposed to facts, or intuition versus reasoning; yet, curiously, often seized upon their chance remarks or sudden insights to set him upon the right track.

Although many of his most challenging or *outré* cases came to him as appeals from the weaker sex, I always felt that Holmes undertook them hesitantly, with an air of reluctant indulgence. Many times, I regret to acknowledge, I have had to smooth the ruffled feathers of an aspiring client, advised by my friend to seek the aid of a clergyman, a policeman, or an elder brother.

Such, I feared, was the situation one fresh spring morning when I returned to Baker Street to find a plumpish, middle-aged lady, with a deeply blushing face and heavy, nervous breathing, in consultation with Sherlock Holmes. One look at my friend's knitted brows and silently drumming fingers, as they stretched along the mantle-piece, showed that here was a client whose case, or perhaps her manner of relating it, had failed to excite the detective's interest.

"Ah, Watson, thank goodness!" cried my friend as I entered the room. "Watson, this is Mrs Hope-Mapperly. Mrs Hope-Mapperly, this is my good friend and colleague Dr Watson. Watson, I fear *Mr* Hope Mapperly has had the misfortune to have himself arrested for spying…but, as Mrs Hope Mapperly has been telling me for the past forty-five minutes, the charge is an absurd one and will assuredly soon be dropped."

Mrs Hope-Mapperly here emitted a curious, high-pitched squeak but as she made no other attempt to speak,

Holmes continued: "I have advised her as much and assured her that should further evidence come to light…"

"There is *some* evidence then?" I interrupted. Holmes and our visitor both turned to face me; my friend's eyebrow raised in amused surprise and Mrs Hope-Mapperly's face alight with what I took to be gratitude, or perhaps a mixture of surprise and delight. Clearly, Holmes had not given Mrs Hope-Mapperly an easy time.

"There is," replied Holmes, slumping into his armchair, his face turned away from us.

Mrs Hope-Mapperly coughed and began her story again. She expressed herself well enough but her voice was monotonous and her nervousness made her almost gasp occasionally for breath. She sat upon our chaise-longue, almost hugging herself with fear, as though she were subject to interrogation by the Inquisition of Spain rather than London's foremost detective and a middle-aged medical man.

"It is my husband," she began, "my poor husband." Holmes waved his hand airily, as though permitting her to continue, and closed his eyes. I smiled some encouragement at Mrs Hope-Mapperly but she simply squeezed herself tighter and began to gabble her story, ever faster and more breathlessly.

"My husband is a good man, Dr Watson. A reliable servant of Tarr & Company and a good husband to me. Tarr & Company are the armaments people, with works beside the arsenal in Woolwich and in the dockyards at Chatham. My husband has been with Tarr's for the best part of twenty years. He is hard working and trustworthy. His reliability has never yet been questioned. Not until a month ago."

As Mrs Hope-Mapperly took a particularly deep gulp of air, I seized the opportunity to ask in what capacity her husband was employed by Tarr's; whom I knew well as manufacturer of every item of military equipment from machine guns and rifles to armour plate and submarines.

"He is in their design works Dr Watson. I am sure he must be important but he doesn't tell me anything about it. He says I wouldn't understand…"

(A snort from Holmes followed this confession).

"…and that it would be a breach of trust for him to say. I imagine it is secret work of national importance. I imagine my Alfred carries worries that would burden the Prime Minister… but until last month he was as light hearted as a newly-wed and as chirpy as a sparrow."

"What has happened then?" I asked.

"Oh, Dr Watson. It was that horrible submarine. He was trapped for nearly two days underwater in that ghastly steel cigar. Something about tanks of air and leaking valves."

"I thought your husband never spoke to you about his work?" I queried - and instantly regretted doing so, as Mrs Hope-Mapperly coloured bright red again and began to huff and puff in her distress.

"I know this only because…because…because Alfred often talks in his sleep. Sometimes he even mutters away when he dozes after dinner in his chair. He hates to do it but he can't help himself; being asleep you see… Anyway, the horror of that accident was acted out night after night. My poor husband, his brow glistening and his arms groping in the darkness for valves or handles. I don't know. It is horrible, Dr Watson, horrible!"

"Indeed," I reassured her, "but who has accused your husband of spying?"

"Well," continued our guest, "poor Alfred wasn't the same after that submarine business. They dredged them all out in the end. All four of them were safe but while the others went meek as anything to hospital, Alfred went back to work. He wouldn't talk about it and he wouldn't let anyone else talk either."

Mrs Hope-Mapperly dabbed at her reddened eyes with a handkerchief and continued between sobs.

"The next I knew was when they brought him home. It seems he'd gone down to the dockyard in Chatham and somehow got into a fight. My Alfred in a fight! It can't be true! Anyway, they brought him home and he had a tussle with the docks policeman then. It isn't Alfred, Dr Watson, it really isn't."

A deep sigh from Holmes, still draped along the mantelpiece, told me this was well-trodden ground. Further exploration of it was suddenly halted however by a furious banging at our street door and raised voices in the hall. Footsteps and further knocking presaged the arrival of two top-hatted gentlemen and the (to us) familiar figure of Inspector Culpepper, like a pocket-Hercules in his tight tweed jacket and low-crowned bowler.

Culpepper strode into our room and pointed to Mrs Hope-Mapperly, who shrivelled even tighter into herself and emitted a series of shrill gasps.

"Not another word, Mrs Hope-Mapperly," snarled the inspector, as he glanced around our room like a lion-tamer who has momentarily misplaced his lion, yet knows it to be somewhere at hand.

"I think we've bothered these gentlemen enough. Perhaps you'd like to come with us. You can take us to your husband. How would that be, eh?"

"Oh, I think not" replied Holmes simply and dispassionately. "Mrs Hope-Mapperly is about to enjoy a cup of tea with us…" Here Holmes strode swiftly to the door, which he flung open again to bellow down to Mrs Hudson for tea and cake.

"There," smiled Holmes, as though the matter were decided, "pray seat yourselves, gentlemen, and we can, perhaps, settle this matter to everyone's satisfaction." With a few simple gestures and a broad smile to Mrs Hope-

Mapperly, Holmes rearranged our seating, so that she took his chair and the three 'official' visitors sat tightly together on our chaise-longue. Holmes then resumed his place at the fireside, where he chatted idly about the weather and the prospects for a fine season until Mrs Hudson had delivered tea and cakes and withdrawn.

Then, his eyes for the first time bright with interest, Holmes rubbed his hands together and addressed himself to the tallest of the top-hatted gentlemen.

"Perhaps we should begin with introductions. Mrs Hope-Mapperly you clearly already know. I am Sherlock Holmes and this is my friend and colleague, Dr Watson."

The tall gentleman, wedged between his associates, his top hat now balanced upon his knees, responded with a slight cough and then spoke in a dry, nasal voice: "My name is Rycraft. I and my colleague here are from the War Department. The inspector I believe you know."

"No, no. That will not suffice. You would have us take you for lowly clerks but that cannot be. Rycraft may be your name," replied Holmes, "but as I last saw you in the library of the Diogenese Club, where, I fancy only a Permanent Secretary *at the least* would dare apply for membership; I suspect we have a delegation from the highest levels of government, Watson."

Rycraft smiled and wriggled slightly, either in his embarrassment or perhaps in an effort to free his elbows from the close proximity of his colleagues, closely packed upon our seat.

"You are quite correct, Mr Holmes. I am indeed a Principal Secretary at the War Office. I am greatly concerned with the case of Alfred Hope-Mapperly, who has access to vital secrets, has been acting erratically (to say the least) and has now escaped from protective custody…"

"Ha! So he has eluded you again!" barked out Sherlock Holmes.

"Indeed," continued Rycraft imperturbably, "You can readily imagine, therefore, why I am anxious to secure Mrs Hope-Mapperly and to be away and about my business. Tea and cake would be delightful but really I cannot spare the time."

The Civil Servant then made an effort to rise (which was not so easy due to the closeness of his colleagues) but Holmes held out his arm to stay the movement.

"We are all busy, sir. Now why should the case of a lowly clerk from Tarr and Company interest you?"

Rycraft sighed and drew a thick blue envelope from an inner pocket of his frock coat. He spread the papers it contained across the top of his hat and studied them for a moment. Then, having apparently made himself master of his brief, Rycraft launched into a lengthy exposition. It was an account worthy of Holmes himself: factual, clear and devoid of extraneous data.

"Alfred Hope-Mapperly is in fact chief design draughtsman for Tarr and Company, working closely with both the War Office and Admiralty. For twelve years he has been responsible for (or at the least has had a hand in) every major patent and development of the company from their new armour-piercing shells, to the turret rotating motors on the new battleships. You've perhaps read of the latest gear for synchronising searchlights and quick-firing guns on our torpedo-boat destroyers? Well, it is a largely Hope-Mapperly design; as are the latest 4.7 inch fuses and the simplified clinometers for the Artillery. Believe me, Hope-Mapperly, in his modest way, is a national treasure."

"Why then this talk of spying?" I asked.

"It is Hope-Mapperly's own behaviour." Rycraft pushed aside the top paper with an outstretched finger. "On the first of this month he was at the Chatham dockyard. He went down with the experimental submersible and was trapped underwater for fifty-eight hours. It was cold and dark. They were hungry but had drinking water enough. On the third of the month they were rescued; yet Hope-Mapperly declined medical treatment and instead went home."

"The next day, the fourth, he returned to Chatham by train. He ascended by hydraulic lift to inspect secret gunnery control equipment high on the masts of the new battleship, currently being fitted-out there. There was some delay and Hope-Mapperly violently assaulted the lift operator and a yard foreman who attempted to intervene."

"He was sent home by train, with a company policeman. From the station they took a closed cab. Hope-Mapperly was quiet at first, even drowsy, but after only a few hundred yards Hope-Mapperly insisted upon stopping the cab and walking the rest of the way. The policeman attempted to follow but lost Hope-Mapperly in the crowds."

Rycraft paused briefly and sifted through his papers once more.

"Two days later Hope-Mapperly was summoned again to the new warship. He refused, with some strong language, to enter the forward gun turret, which was the cause of some difficulty in the works. Once again, he left the dockyard in some haste and could not be followed."

Rycraft sucked his teeth and pushed another paper forward across his top-hat.

"A week ago he was asked to attend the gunnery range at Whale Island. There was an altercation there too. This time Hope-Mapperly forced an abrupt halt to the gunnery demonstration by storming out of the safety hut after yet another violent altercation with the Royal Marine Artillery officers present. There was talk of raised voices and fisticuffs and once again Hope-Mapperly disappeared into Portsmouth."

"I'd like him safely locked up…" began Inspector Culpepper grimly but he was silenced by Rycraft, who laid his hand upon the inspector's sleeve.

"Our principal concern is for Hope-Mapperly's welfare. He is a vital man for us. His knowledge and understanding is second to none. Sadly," said Rycraft with a sigh, "such skills make him a valuable man for our nation's rivals too."

"You believe then," said I, "that Hope-Mapperly has eluded your men to put himself into the hands of enemy agents?"

"It is conceivable," replied Rycraft sadly, "and that possibility is enough for us to take certain safeguards."

Further discussion was cut short at that moment by the sudden, noisy, arrival of a police sergeant at our street door. After a few moments, the sergeant was shown in by Mrs Hudson. He whispered briefly into the ear of Culpepper, who conferred with Rycraft and his associate. The inspector rose to speak but once again Rycraft laid a restraining arm across his: "It would appear that Mr Hope-Mapperly has been traced. He was 'picked-up', I hesitate to say 'arrested', half an hour ago, in Belgravia; a short distance from the German, Austrian and Italian embassies."

Rycraft nodded to Holmes and me and motioned to the inspector to bring Mrs Hope-Mapperly.

"We need trouble you no further Mr Holmes. Mrs Hope-Mapperly's presence will greatly assist our enquiries. Good day gentlemen."

Holmes remained leaning against our fire-place; an enigmatic smile upon his lips. I followed our visitors to the top of our stairs however and assured Mrs Hope-Mapperly that we would not abandon her.

"All will be well, I assure you…" I stammered, "put your faith in Sherlock Holmes."

"Some hope" replied Inspector Culpepper grimly.

I returned to our sitting room, to find Holmes staring out of the window at the four-wheeler into which our visitors were, at that very moment, climbing.

"Is there nothing we can do?" I said.

"Do, Watson? I fancy the solution to this mystery – the curious conduct of Mr Alfred Hope-Mapperly – lies more in your sphere than mine."

"Really?" I asked.

"Ah, Watson, think of the train of events as a medical man, rather than a detective. Trace the symptoms back to their root cause. Hope-Mapperly fights his way from a lift, a cab, a gun turret, and finally a shell-proof hut. Then he dashes off and cannot be found – until he is run to earth, I suspect, in one of the nearby parks and gardens. There are your symptoms; now, what is the cause?"

"The submersible!" I cried. "Of course! Two days trapped in the cold and dark of that underwater coffin! It is a clear case. Hope-Mapperly is suffering from delayed shock and claustrophobia. Who wouldn't, in such circumstances, react against the danger of getting trapped in a lift, or locked into a hut. Why? It is obvious!"

"Indeed Watson" observed my friend wistfully, "obvious."

"Then, I suppose there is little more that we can do. Rycraft will detain Hope-Mapperly for his own good and seek medical help for him, while at the same time ensuring that there is no danger of foreign agents interfering while Hope-Mapperly's defences are weakened."

"There is certainly little to be done this evening. I suggest that we repair to the Strand for dinner and then see what tickets may be had at the opera."

* * *

I was woken the next morning by Sherlock Holmes, who tapped insistently at my bedroom door and urged me to dress in haste, as Mrs Hope-Mapperly was awaiting us in our sitting room. I joined Holmes and his client within a few minutes; dressed but unshaven. Mrs Hudson had already brought up some tea and toast and was coaxing some warmth from the fire.

"Thank you Mrs Hudson" said Holmes, helping her to her feet, and propelling our landlady from the room. "Now, Mrs Hope-Mapperly, what news did the telegram boy bring?"

"Mr Holmes?" asked our visitor, perplexed.

"I see the envelope protruding from your coat pocket…and, really, what else could cause you to hasten here at so early an hour?"

"Oh, yes," replied Mrs Hope-Mapperly, her face downcast and gloomy. "Here is the telegram…"

Sherlock Holmes hastily extracted the telegram form and tutted loudly. "Oh dear me, Watson. It seems this poor lady's husband has tried to take his own life."

Holmes paused for a moment and stroked the empty envelope thoughtfully against his chin. Suddenly he turned to our client.

"Mrs Hope-Mapperly, I take it that your husband is not the sort to panic…to, shall we say, take his own life as a way out of a difficult situation?"

"Certainly not, Mr Holmes, I am shocked that you should even…"

"Quite so," interrupted my friend. "Inspector Culpepper will no doubt regard an attempted suicide as proof of guilt. We must seek another motive. Come Watson! We shall go immediately to the police station. Mrs Hope-Mapperly, I beg you to return home. Trust us and await our news."

Leaving Mrs Hope-Mapperly to the tender care of Mrs Hudson, Holmes and I dashed into Baker Street, hailed a cab and within a few minutes were bowling down the Marylebone Road towards Culpepper's police station. As luck would have it, we were too late; Hope-Mapperly having been declared fit to travel by a police doctor and carried off by Rycraft in a four-wheeler, straight-jacketed and between two burly policemen.

To add to our chagrin, we ran into Culpepper, returning to the police station just as we were leaving it.

"Good morning Mr Holmes…and Dr Watson," he cried cheerily, his cherubic and well-scrubbed face beaming with pleasure at what he perceived to be our discomfort.

"I'm afraid you've missed our little spy. Mr Rycraft took him off an hour ago. Sharp fellow that Rycraft. Still, I'm not sure he is quite right in having Hope-Mapperly down as ill rather than criminal." Here, Culpepper pushed his hat back and tapped his forehead: "he thinks him more in your line, doctor, than mine, eh?"

I was inclined to let Culpepper have his moment of pleasure but my friend reacted angrily.

"Where has Hope-Mapperly been taken?" snapped Holmes. "Quickly man! Do you know?"

"Of course I know" replied Culpepper, now rather less sure of himself.

"Well?"

"Rycraft told Hope-Mapperly before breakfast that he would have to make another visit to some mental specialist."

"*Another* visit?" barked Holmes. "Did he name him? And was Hope-Mapperly told before or after he attempted to take his own life?"

The detective's lips formed words but none came.

"Well man?" barked Holmes.

"Er…it was before," replied Culpepper, clearly alarmed at my friend's anxiety.

"And what do you mean by *another* visit to a mental specialist?"

Culpepper swallowed hard and ran a finger around the inside of his collar before answering. "Well, it was Rycraft's idea. He reckoned Hope-Mapperly was er…unbalanced by sinking in the submarine and he took him to a top bloke in Harley Street. It was on the recommendation of our police doctor. I gather he had some success and requested another session."

"A specialist, Watson. Clearly they value Hope-Mapperley rather more highly than it appeared earlier."

"What was his name," I asked, "…this specialist?"

Culpepper gulped and appeared to make some mental effort. After at least half a minute's thought, he muttered doubtfully "Strawberry".

"Not Straubenzee!" I ejaculated. "They certainly do value Hope-Mapperley if they're sending him to Straubenzee."

Holmes raised his eyebrows and gestured that he would know more.

"Well," I continued, "Straubenzee is a society doctor; his patients are worn-out politicians and hysterical countesses. I can't say much beyond what I hear from colleagues and I fear there is a deal of professional jealousy in the stories they tell. In general, Straubenzee is highly regarded and has had considerable success in cases of shock, or where physical effects are brought on by mental *trauma*…as they call it. I read a very advanced paper of his last year dealing with hypnotism in…"

"Come!" bellowed Holmes, storming out of the police station. "Hurry! Culpepper – a cab! Quickly!"

We were in Harley Street within ten minutes. I paid our fare, while Holmes dashed for an elegant portal, which bore the brass plate of Dr Emerich Straubenzee. I too entered, closely pursued by Inspector Culpepper and a red-faced, puffing constable.

Inside, all was confusion. Rycraft had clearly been waiting in Straubenzee's anteroom, with another constable, while Hope-Mapperly received his treatment. Both were on their feet, neither quite comprehending Holmes's swift passage past them into Straubenzee's consulting room.

"What on earth is going on?" appealed Rycraft as Culpepper and I entered. The principal secretary seemed outraged: "I told Holmes that Straubenzee was trying mesmerism and that he should not enter. He replied that it was the very reason he should. He then burst straight in on them. Now, what in heaven's name could justify such behaviour?"

"This!" replied Holmes swinging through the consulting room door and flinging down a red-leather bound notebook before the civil servant. Rycraft picked up the book and read; the blood draining from his face as he did so.

I was fully occupied then with Hope-Mapperly, whose physical and mental state gave me great cause for concern. It was not until late that evening then, as Holmes and I lit our post-prandial cigars, that I was able to ask for a full explanation of the case.

"What was in the notebook?" I asked.

"It was a full account of the failings of the latest model of Whitehead torpedo and several possible solutions," replied Holmes, "I am sure you would hardly expect me to give it you word for word."

"Indeed not...but how on earth did you know that Hope-Mapperly was the victim rather than perpetrator?"

"I simply considered the same facts from a different perspective, Watson. To Culpepper, Hope-Mapperly's attempted suicide was proof of guilt. I merely considered another option. We knew Hope-Mapperly spoke in his sleep and at the police station we learned that he was being forced into a series of sessions of hypnosis as a treatment. At that point Hope-Mapperly came into focus as an honest man, driven to take a fatal step as the only means of ensuring his own silence."

Holmes's cigar glowed in the dark and he exhaled a bluish cloud of smoke towards the ceiling.

"I couldn't be sure, Watson, but I apprehended the danger and made haste in case I was right. The mention of mesmerism was enough for me. I burst in on Straubenzee and his assistant, who fled through the rear of the building; leaving proof of their guilt in the form of that notebook."

"What of Rycraft?" I asked: "was he part of the conspiracy?"

"More fool than knave I fancy," murmured Holmes, already drifting off into his own thoughts.

The case was firmly closed a week later. Holmes returned from lunch with his brother at the Diogenes Club. His face, as he hung up his hat in our hall, wore that enigmatic smile which I often detected when my friend pondered upon the irony of the world.

"You will appreciate this, Watson," he smiled. "Tomorrow's newspapers will carry a notice that the eminent doctor, Emerich Straubenzee, late of Harley Street, has returned to Vienna to continue his studies."

"He escaped then?" I asked.

"Not a bit of it, Watson. As brother Mycroft engagingly put it; no physician whose clients include members of the royal family and government front bench, can safely be put on trial. There is no knowing what they might say!"

"My word," was all I could respond. "But Holmes, what of Hope-Mapperly and Rycraft?"

"Hope-Mapperly is a vital man and a proven patriot. I understand he tried desperately to explain his weakness to Rycraft and the fool brushed aside the warning as the ravings of a sick man. That he was prepared even to take his own life in order to deny vital secrets to our nation's enemies proves his worth. He can be assured of promotion if he recovers and a fine pension if not."

"As for Rycraft, I can say only this. I enquired after him with the porter at the Diogenese Club…"

Here Holmes's cigar glowed again.

"…And they affected never to have heard the name!"

The Case of the bewildered Banker

My friend, Mr Sherlock Holmes, was by no means the ideal man with whom to share lodgings. His untidiness usually did not trouble me, as I scarcely excelled in that line myself. His eccentric fiddle-playing and chemical experiments were trying but generally short-lived but his moods, particularly the black depressions which occasionally gripped him, were more disturbing.

I was always happy therefore to see Holmes immersed in work. His energetic pursuit of a case, or any intellectual pastime, was always welcome as an antidote to the lethargy and near despair which seemed to accompany unemployment.

At times I marvelled as Holmes took two or even three clients on at a time. Often they brought trivial matters requiring merely a few hours' thought, perhaps a day at the British Museum's Reading Room, or a visit to the offices of a shipping line. In any case my friend seemed able to juggle matters, so that one puzzle could safely be left simmering, whilst he busily stirred new ingredients into another.

On only two or three occasions can I recall Sherlock Holmes confessing to being overwhelmed – or, at least, unable to cope alone. There was the affair of the Baskervilles in Devon, when pressing business kept him in London; though I recall that the need to despatch me alone to Dartmoor was in part a ruse in order to steal a march on our foe.

Another was shortly after the melancholy case of the Cushing family, late in the summer of '88. I recollect that my friend Holmes was pursuing an eloped daughter of the Earl of Ditchwater, whilst he was also investigating forged local government bonds, when an urgent request for help reached him from a foreign head of state. It was not a matter of great importance – indeed, the full facts of the case now elude me (such was their lack of interest) but it was accompanied with an appeal from a quarter so exalted as not to be denied.

Even so, I was surprised one morning to find Holmes in a somewhat anxious state. He had burst in upon my breakfast, pouring out and draining with one gulp my cup of Irish breakfast tea.

"Ah!" he gasped. "Admirably refreshing, Watson."
"I'll send for more," I offered, only slightly put out (as there was but one cup on the table).

"No, no Watson," he replied, "I am afraid I have only come in for a clean collar and a glance at the post. I am rather hopeful of a letter from Monaco."

"Nothing so exotic this morning" I responded, handing him a couple of unremarkable looking envelopes. One of the envelopes Holmes cast aside with a sigh, the other he tore open with my butter knife. He glanced at the contents with ill-concealed distaste. He then tossed both letter and envelope (the latter with a long smear of yellow butter) into my lap.

"Yet another cry for help, Watson. A Mr. Nevinson Dunlop proposes to call upon me at eleven of the clock." Holmes glanced at his watch, snapping it shut with a grimace.

"Alas, I shall be in Chancery Lane." He paused for a second's thought: "I have it! You will take the case, or at least interview Mr Nevison Dunlop and see whether there is one. His letter, as always, tells us nothing of value beyond that its writer fancies the matter to be important. You, Watson, can sift this fellow's corn and, if you would be so kind, blow the chaff from the wheat."

"If I can be of help…" I replied, though in truth I had planned a rather less taxing morning for myself.

"Capital. Well, I must seize that collar and be away. I depend upon you Watson."

* * *

In fact, Mr James Nevinson-Dunlop, Accountant and Business Promoter (as his stationery had announced) arrived forty minutes early and missed Sherlock Holmes, who had decided that a shave as well as fresh collar was required, by a mere quarter of an hour.

I was gazing down into the bustle of Baker Street, when I saw his cab arrive. That the passenger sought *our* door was clear enough. I've seen it often enough. The cab progressed up the street in fits and starts, as both passenger and cabbie read the house numbers. Then, out leapt the shiniest, most stylish silk top hat I had seen since the affair of the Naval Treaty. Finally, there was an altercation over the fare, which convinced me that, early though it was, here was my 'Accountant and Business Promoter'.

Within two minutes the street doorbell rang and James Nevinson-Dunlop was shown into our sitting room. He was an unremarkable man of middle height and build, clean-shaven and with his hair oiled and parted in the centre. I could see nothing, beside a particularly gaudy tie-pin to set him apart from the run of well-dressed, middle-aged City men.

If he was disappointed to find Holmes absent, Mr Nevinson-Dunlop was good enough to conceal the fact. Indeed, if anything, he affected to be pleased. He spoke with a slight Scottish accent and even slighter stammer, which softened a rather urgent, even impatient manner.

"I confess I am sorry to find Mr Holmes o-otherwise engaged," he said, leaning forward from our best armchair. "I would have welcomed the chance to see a famous detective in action. However, to see Dr. Watson is hardly less i-i-impressive and, I rather suspect that I have before me the more d-dogged half of the 'team'. You'll deny it, of course, b-but I know modesty when I see it and I appreciate it when I do."

"I am afraid you exaggerate my role in Mr Holmes's investigations," I protested, "though I believe that he does find my notes useful on occasion and if I can save him time now, by taking down the particulars of your problem, it may lead to a speedier resolution of the case."

"Fair enough!" ejaculated the Accountant and Business Promoter, slapping his knees. "I'll g-give you the facts of the case and you can interpret them for Mr Holmes. I confess I am much perturbed and any resolution or reassurance will be w-welcome indeed."

I sat with my notebook and silver pencil to hand, while Nevinson-Dunlop pondered briefly where to begin.

"I have a number of business interests," he began after nearly a minute's thought. "Mostly stocks and sh-shares, though I have also invested my own and others' money in a variety of ventures; from the projected Channel Tunnel to departmental stores and new chemical dyes. Believe me, there are f-fortunes to be made through careful, early investments. Get into a concern at birth and p-pennies become guineas as it grows."

I nodded and wrote "speculator" in my notebook.

"Now, you'll see why returns at f-first may be low," continued Nevinson-Dunlop, nervously fingering the brim of his silk hat; "and why I took a partner to share the strain. A man by the name of Fullager, Elijah Fullager."

I wrote: "In financial trouble".

"For two years my partner and I have ridden the crest of the wave. We were in on Orinoco g-guano; and Palatinate Zinc was largely our doing – though we s-sold out last year with two-hundred per-cent profits. Now, we are considering a venture, a really big thing, north of the border. It quite takes all our gains, all our capital and a little besides – but that's n-nothing unusual in our business. It is well worth while and p-perfectly secured."

"I cannot quite see how Mr Holmes and I might be of use to you," said I, as my visitor paused for breath and thought.

"No indeed," he replied, "but the b-background is important I'm sure."

"Of course" I murmured.

"Well," Nevinson-Dunlop continued, "three days ago, I lunched with Fullager to iron-out one or two minor details of the business. Instead of signing it all off however, Elijah presented me with a cheque for nearly fifteen thousand pounds and told me our firm was dissolved."

"Was the cheque good?" I asked.

My visitor smiled. "I had the same thought, Dr Watson; but my bank told me yesterday morning that all was well and that the cheque had cleared. I went to Fullager's lodgings only to be told that he had 'come into money' and departed for a continental holiday. The best they could offer by way of a forwarding address was *poste restante* in Nice. It just isn't Elijah's way, Dr Watson, it really isn't. The fifteen thousand pounds notwithstanding, I remain desperately unhappy at this state of affairs. Something is the matter, I know it is."

I thought for a moment, pondering what Holmes would do or ask. Finally, I rose to my feet and shook hands with my client.

"I'll look into the matter," was all I could think to say, "I shall need full particulars of Elijah Fullager and your business interests. I presume you are proceeding with the Scottish venture alone now?"

Nevinson-Dunlop paused in the doorway, his face a study in concern. "I have written the details here in a memorandum. As for our business scheme; it is quite abandoned. Elijah had the whole affair entirely in his hands.

My part was to raise the capital down here, while he smoothed our path north of the border. I know next to nothing and he left, saying that was quite the best way and that I should leave well alone. Those were his very words, Dr Watson, he said 'take the money and leave well alone.' "

* * *

I dined with Holmes that evening at Baker Street. It was a hasty meal, with barely time for a cigar together afterwards before he dashed out again. My outline of the Fullager case seemed to arouse little interest.

"My dear Watson," said my friend with a wink, "you are easily up to this business. Detective work is far more diligence than brilliance! My advice is to look to the financial 'papers. Devour them! This bewildered banker of yours says in his note that he and Fullager formed their 'Anglo-Caledonian Trading Company' in November last year. My advice is to scan the financial papers for the fortnight before. See what was on offer then in North Britain!"

Well might Mr Sherlock Holmes wink! Many a time have I written that he returned home after long hours at the British Library, or some newspaper office or other. Little did I imagine myself slowly turning wearisome page after wearisome page in pursuit of I knew not what.

Still, Holmes was proved right at last. Full three weeks' worth of commercial reporting after I began my search, I found the notice which must have attracted the attention of Elijah Fullager's astute financial eye. It was for a lower Clyde wharf, its equipment, and associated land, buildings and railway sidings.

A further morning's work amongst the records first of Companies' House and then the *Edinburgh Gazette* added meat to the bare bones. It concerned Drummuir Wharf.

Fullager, I learned, had snapped up the rare prize, dropped by a bankrupt Glasgow jute dealer, of a prime Clydeside dock; ripe for development and perfect after a little artful dredging, for Irish or Isle of Man ferries, or even ocean-going vessels of up to twenty-thousand tons.

Holmes's absence from our lodgings that evening, robbed me of the satisfaction of reporting my success in person. Glad to be rid of a case which, more than any other, had revived the gnawing back pain of my old Afghanistan wound, I cheerfully penned a full account of my research and propped it beside Holmes's pipes upon the mantelpiece in our sitting room.

My disappointment the following morning was profound however, when I discovered my report amongst the cold remnants of my absent friend's long abandoned breakfast, bearing the scrawled addendum: *"Well done Watson. Capital work. Now – cui bono? There is a dining-car express from Euston at 1.30."*

Well might Holmes ask who would benefit from the sudden collapse of a partnership; I knew for certain it was not me! Nevertheless, I packed a Gladstone bag and strolled to Euston Station, happy to take advantage of a fresh breeze, which I hoped might promote thoughts of the case.

Alas, inspiration seemed to have deserted me. I lunched well and dozed over a novel from the station bookstall as the mountains of the Lake District and then the melancholy hills of lowland Scotland passed by my window. From Penrith the view was besmirched by drizzle, which shrouded the distant views in mist and sent raindrops coursing across the glass.

The dismal weather did not lower my spirits however. Rather it concentrated my thoughts upon the case and though, I confess, I came to no more solid conclusion than I had walking up Baker Street; I determined to wrench the truth from the mystery and to impress Holmes with my worth.

My determination had not in the least diminished by the following morning, when I stepped out of my hotel into the bright sunshine of a new day. At the Low Level station I found that I had over an hour to wait, as the next trains out towards Helensburgh were either workmen's, with nothing but third class, or the Boat Express, which did not stop at Blairbeg; the nearest station to Fullager's wharf.

The station bar was open, however, and the hour's delay did not pass unpleasantly. Finally, just after eleven-thirty my train shook itself free of Glasgow's western suburbs and I was treated to a truly stunning view of the River Clyde, its blue waters glittering in the benevolent sunshine. The crag of Dumbarton came and went and the smoke of Port Glasgow hove into sight two or three miles across the water.

At twenty minutes to one my train slithered to a halt at Blairbeg, where the locomotive let off steam with a sigh that echoed my own. The place was almost deserted. I stood alone on the wooden platform, uncertain which way to go, or to whom I might present my ticket and ask. After a minute or two, the train eased itself out of the station and from the cloud of smoke and steam stepped an elderly employee of the North British Railway.

"Can you direct me to Drummuir Wharf?" I asked, after showing my ticket.
"Drummuir Wharf?" the fellow exclaimed, "I wouldn't go there if I were you, sir. If it is walking, or fishing, or shooting you're after I'd try up the line beyond Helensburgh. There's a fine hotel in the town and plenty of transport for day trippers."

"But I'm not here for sport," I replied. "I'm on business and I want the Drummuir Wharf, if you'd be kind enough to point me in the right direction. Is it far? Is there a dog-cart or fly I can hire?"

"You can walk easy enough," responded the porter. "It is half a mile, no more, but it's a wee bit muddy this time of year and you'll no be welcome when you get there."

"I'll take that risk," said I forcefully and the railwayman shrugged and gave me the directions I needed.

The track was rutted and muddy but the way was clear enough. Indeed, it bore clear signs of many heavily-laden vehicles, all making their way towards the river. At several points deep ruts had been recently filled with gravel and at one particularly sharp turn, I detected damage to the verge and a fence which suggested that some wagon or other had met with an accident. Deep gouges showed in the soft turf that something long and sharp-edged had fallen heavily from the trackway.

After a few more minutes' walk I clearly heard a steam whistle close by, though whether from a boat on the river or an engine ashore I could not tell. At last I turned a corner and saw to my left, the broad expanse of the Clyde, between two stands of timber. My road ahead, however, was blocked by a tall and stout wooden fence and a gate to match.

Lounging beside the gate were two bruisers in blue seamen's jerseys, who stood upright with folded arms as I approached. When the larger of the two spoke, I was astonished to hear not the local brogue but a Cornish accent.

"Yes, matey? Lost are we?"

"Not in the least," I responded. "I would like access to Drummuir Wharf if you have no objection."

"Not possible, sir, I'm afraid," said the other in an equally out of place voice; possibly Norfolk or Suffolk, I am unsure.

"Might I see the man in charge?"

"Not here, sir, and left clear orders to see off sightseers."

I remonstrated for a few minutes more but could see I was wasting my time. Throughout our conversation, if I can so dignify the exchange, I heard shouts of workmen, the clang of tools upon metal and a rhythmic thudding, which I put down to a pile-driver embedding timber baulks in the riverbank.

What is more, I had noticed a stretch of the fence down by the river, where the timber seemed to have come loose or been damaged, and I resolved to return later that evening perhaps when I might manage to scramble up or over, to see what was going on at Drummuir Wharf. I felt that to be the course of action Sherlock Holmes would take and, candidly, I could think of no other.

Fortune here smiled upon me. Loathe to return to the gain-sayer at the railway halt, I decided to turn northwards up the Clyde and within fifteen minutes' march I came upon first the highroad and then a pleasing inn, which advertised not only local ales but also food.

Mindful of my friend Holmes's dictum that a local public house is the fount of all gossip, I decided to eat first and then, as a parting shot, to ask about the wharf. At first mine host shook his head, declaring that he was "of course mindful that the old place is buzzing again" but that the workmen kept themselves entirely to themselves and that "besides the young lieutenant and the American" they brought no business to the inn.

I must confess that when I stepped outside, I stood deep in thought for well over a minute before stepping out for Craigendoran, where I hoped the ferry traffic would give me camouflage enough before returning that evening.

"The young lieutenant and the American" echoed and re-echoed as I walked. What could it mean? What were they doing at Drummuir and what could it possibly have to do with Elijah Fullager and poor Nevinson-Dunlop?

I spent a surprisingly agreeable afternoon at Craigendoran, watching the river traffic and the ferry to the Isles arrive and depart, with its intriguing mix of passengers, luggage and livestock. At six I was rested, fed and watered and eager to return for round-two at Drummuir. The weather had turned colder and a little wetter but this, I decided, could only aid my endeavours and I smiled silently to myself as I climbed aboard a hired dog-cart for the six or seven miles back to the wharf.

It was dusk and a misty, rainy evening when I left my conveyance on the high road beside the inn to walk down to the wharf. The sun had already taken cover behind the mountains of Bute but its light still showed as a faint halo as I plunged through the long grass beside the rutted riverside track. I reached the long perimeter fence just as night relieved the sentinel of dusk and the shadows deepened into darkness.

Ahead of me all was quiet. The boom of the pile-driver (if that is what it was) had ceased and I could detect nothing beside a few voices and, once, as I waited in the shadow of the fence, the scent of strong tobacco on the night air. I sat beneath the fence for nearly an hour, listening and watching, until all was quite quiet.

At length I began to crawl along the fence, feeling - as much as looking - for the weak point I had identified that afternoon. After a few anxious minutes, I found it and confirmed that my first suspicions had been true. The fence was split and by working away at a bolt-hole, I was quickly able to peer through. I saw...nothing. A few feet in front of the fence was a long, low building which wholly obscured my view.

After a moment's thought I decided that Holmes would scarcely be deflected by such a set back and I resolved to climb over and explore. It was easier said than done but after a couple of false starts I managed to scale the fence and actually leaped onto the roof of the low building which had scuppered my original plan.

I scrambled down and began to investigate. The site had been cleared and from what I could see, the original wharf had been extended and renewed. Several large machines stood idle in the darkness and a small dredger lay tied up alongside the dock. There *was* a pile-driver beside the river and another steam engine stood in a lean-to, surrounded by piles of sawn timber. Mysterious dark mounds proved, on closer inspection, to be stores of some sort, covered with grey-green tarpaulins.

As I approached the farther edge of the wharf, I heard low voices and then saw the light from several oil lamps. A small group of four or five was standing at the water's edge, a few yards from where the dredger had scooped and dumped a long mound of gravel and mud. The men were intently watching the now dark river, its oily black surface creased by occasional ripples, which caught the lamp or possibly moon-light.

I crept closer, also watching the water. My eyes narrowed as I desperately sought some sign of what held their attention. Suddenly, the river belched forth two or three great bubbles of air, as though a drowning man were in the depths calling for help! The river's surface then seemed to simmer, the oily water rising and writhing; slipping away from first a fin or some other projection and then a broad, glistening black back, as though a vast fish or whale were surfacing at the men's command!

I stepped back in surprise and cried out as I slipped – though whether in shock at the sudden emergence of the monster of the deep or simply in alarm at losing my footing I cannot say. In any case, I was hauled to my feet by two burly workmen and half walked, half carried back to the hut I had first landed upon in my leap from the wall.

I was forced down into a chair and held firmly in place until a tall young man in a worn reefer or pea coat, entered the room and indicated that the grip might be relaxed.

"Well? Who are you?" asked the young fellow, his hands upon his hips. I had begun to respond in the same vein, when another man, older and stockier, entered the hut. He spoke in an unmistakably American accent and seemed rather more angry, or perhaps worried, than his younger companion.

"You're Russian aren't you?" he demanded. "I knew it! I knew they'd be onto us. He must be Russian....or German. Damn it! If the French or Italians have cottoned on to this!"

"Calm yourself," replied the other. "To judge from his tweeds and boots, this is an Englishman and doubtless a loyal one too." He turned to me and smiled, an oddly distracted smile, which I did not find reassuring.

"My name," I retorted, is Dr John Watson and I am not only a loyal Englishman but have proved that loyalty through arduous service on the North West Frontier and in Afghanistan. I demand, rather, to know who you are and what you are doing with Elijah Fullager's wharf?"

For a few seconds there was silence. The most frightening silence I have known. But then, suddenly, the American burst out with a guffaw of laughter.

"Oh my, oh my," he said, "that confounded Fullager again. I told Royston! I told them all we should take his partner into our confidence and buy him out too. I *told* them he wouldn't go quietly!"

"Not our business," snapped the younger man. "Royston's on his way here anyway. He'll decide what to do with Mr Watson here, and you can share your views on Fullager with him when he arrives."

I remained confined to my chair for the best part of an hour until the roving beam of a bright search-light lit up the hut and told me that 'Royston' had arrived by some fast river launch. My surprise was almost complete when the man himself entered the hut…in the uniform of a senior British naval officer.

For a moment or two the new arrival looked me up and down, as though appraising me. Then, suddenly, he drove his right fist into his left hand, as though a decision had forced the physical action. He stepped forward and shook my hand.

"I am Commodore Royston. These gentlemen…", here he gestured to the young man and the American, "are Charles Davidson and Henry Bruce-Partington. You will not have heard of us…"

"But I have," I interrupted, "or at least of Mr Bruce-Partington. The designer of submersible craft, I presume?"

"Perhaps I was wrong," muttered the Commodore, "and you are a spy."

I hastily explained my knowledge, from a case a year before, of the Bruce-Partington plans for submarine vessels.
The Commodore sighed and nodded. "Alas, there are no secrets any more. But I fancy there are still English gentlemen, who may be trusted to keep what they have seen secret; at least until that secret is no longer of importance?"

"There are," I replied, "provided that I am satisfied that your work here is above board, if not above the surface, and that my client (if I can so term him), Mr Nevinson-Dunlop is adequately compensated for his loss and reassured about his missing partner.

"You will be," growled the Commodore, "and so will he. I was mistaken in treating the fellow so cavalierly. We are under pressure, Dr Watson, since the half of the Admiralty which believes in our work is dead against it, while the other half really only fears that it may be true."

The Commodore took my arm and walked me to his launch. Davidson and the American, Bruce-Partington, followed sheepishly behind. He shook my hand and almost whispered in my ear: "Our biggest ally in Whitehall is Mr Mycroft Holmes. I know that means something to you but I beg you to say no more. Preserve our secret; which may save our nation in a few years! Now, *bon voyage* and keep those lips sealed!"

The naval launch raced up river with such speed that I caught the first train of the day to London, though my luggage was left in the care of the Royal Navy, to follow at a slower pace.

I arrived at Baker Street, exhausted, and with my head still reeling at all I had seen and heard. My friend, Sherlock Holmes, was descending the stairs of number 221B as I arrived home. It no longer surprised me that he should be costumed as denizen of London's underworld, nor that he should greet me with a loud cry. We stood briefly together in the hallway of our lodgings.

"Watson! I am delighted to see you back so soon. I fear it must be 'hail and farewell' though, as I am late already! How was Glasgow? Did you solve the case?"

I shook my head sadly. "A failure I'm afraid. Nothing to see up there of any help. It is a dead stop."

Holmes patted my shoulder.
"My dear Watson! You did your best. Don't berate yourself. Even I have been known to fail."

And with that, Holmes slammed the door shut behind him and left.

The Case of the Holy Bones

"The price of toast, my dear Watson, is eternal vigilance. There is simply no other way to ensure the perfect, universal, golden brown colour than to remain for ever at the *qui vive* whilst your bread toasts. Should the attention wander, even for a single second, all may be lost. I have in mind a monograph upon the subject…"

"Thank you Holmes," I replied, "I'll take mine as it comes from Mrs Hudson and be glad not to have to crouch over our fire for hours on end with a toasting fork."

"You may have a point" replied my friend with a deep sigh, rising from our fire and casting the fork, still with its burden of pale, untoasted bread, into the hearth. "I am unconvinced that I actually like toast anyway. Reality never really equals expectation, and the transformation from golden perfection to cold cardboard is far too rapid."

Holmes joined me at our breakfast table, which was cluttered with the remains of our kippers, our newspapers, and that morning's post. For the first breakfast in more than a week, my friend was in a distinctly good humour; his unexpected joviality prompting me into a deduction of my own.

"I perceive that at last you have a promising case. I presume it was brought by the postman."

"Remarkable Watson," Holmes replied, "I see that I must look to my laurels. Meanwhile, I would be obliged if you would look over this and let me know what you make of it." He tossed an envelope across the table to me.

Now, here was the sort of game I enjoyed. I took my time, studying first the address and postmark and then turning the envelope carefully in my hands. I was surprised to see that the flap of the envelope had been sealed with wax as well as gummed down. Holmes was watching me intently.

"Well, what can you deduce from the envelope?" he asked at length.

"Firstly", I replied irritably, "the envelope has been opened using our butter knife."

"Watson! You excel."

"Hmm" I replied. "It is good quality stationery. Someone is out to impress. It was posted yesterday in Sandchester. The address is carefully written, with a newish pen, in blue-black ink. The writing is halting though…"

"Capital, Watson!"

"The writing is that of an educated man but, I suggest, an elderly or infirm one."

"And the seal, Watson, what do you make of that?"

"Ah, the seal. Firstly, it is unnecessary as the gum would have served just as well on its own. Secondly, it is ostentatious – even a little vulgar perhaps. I may be wholly in error here but I would suggest some nouveau-riche tradesman, recently knighted perhaps and anxious that we should all know of it. He is on holiday in Sandchester and has discovered some mystery at his lodgings. Am I right Holmes?"

My friend chortled with amusement: "Indeed you are Watson. Indeed you are."

"Do you know the new-made knight then, Holmes?" I asked.

"Ah, no, forgive me," replied Holmes: "I meant that you are right in thinking yourself 'wholly in error'. However, your mistakes are all understandable and you are quite correct about both stationery and place of postage. As for the seal, it is vesical (a lozenge) in shape and therefore of either a lady, or a religious house. In this case it bears an image of St Margaret spearing a dragon and therefore, it would be reasonable to deduce, originated in the cathedral church of St Margaret at Sandchester."

"Yes, well…" I responded gloomily, at least I was right about the handwriting. An elderly clergyman no doubt…"

"Alas not, Watson. The hand is that of a lady and a young one too, or at least with no physical impairment. What you took for halting decrepitude, is simply hesitancy in writing occasioned, I fancy, from the need to copy my address from some other source."

"At least I noticed the hesitancy" I riposted, nettled by Holmes's apparent assuredness.

"Yes, well done Watson. You have a keen eye for sure but are too easily led astray by the lure of a good story. Let us examine the contents of the envelope. I would greatly value your opinion."

The envelope bulged with a letter (once again on expensive paper) and several newspaper cuttings. I opened the letter first, which was written in the same hand and ink as the envelope, though much more fluently it is true.

The Deanery,
No. 1, The Close
Sandchester

Dear Mr Holmes,

I write to you on behalf of my father, the Dean of Sandchester. He was advised that you might be prepared to help us by Lady Alicia Whittington, who is resident here for the season. I fear my father, being an invalid, is quite upset by the whole business and unequal to the task of setting out what has happened for you.

Mr Holmes, there is more to this than meets the eye and I beg of you to come down to save this

ancient cathedral from a scandal, or worse, which would spell ruin for us all.

The enclosed newspaper clippings will give you the facts of the case. I shall tell you what lies behind them when you arrive. I have taken the liberty of reserving rooms for you and Dr Watson at the Pilgrim's Rest; an ancient inn beside the Close here in Sandchester.

I beg of you to come.

Yours in despair,

Millicent Watts

I folded the letter and looked for reaction to Holmes. He smiled and sat back in his chair, pressing his outstretched fingers together in thought.

"A singularly unhelpful letter for the armchair theorist, eh Watson? I fear we shall have to travel down to Sandchester if we would know more. You had better read us the clippings. We can at least have the 'facts of the case', as Miss Watts puts it, even if we must await the 'more…than meets the eye'."

I turned to the newspaper cuttings. The first was from the *Sandchester Sentry*, a weekly paper, of ten days before. The *Sentry's* architectural correspondent reported the collapse of a small section of the wall of the crypt during building work to repair a crack in the masonry. To the surprise of the workmen and the cathedral's retained architect, the collapse revealed that the wall seemed to serve no architectural purpose, other than to conceal a small chantry chapel and tomb.

Under the headline 'Saint's Relics Revealed' the Sandchester *Evening Post* of two days later was able both to report and speculate more. I turned in my chair to read the significant paragraphs aloud to Holmes, who had abandoned our breakfast table in search of a more comfortable armchair and a meditative cigarette.

> *"The recent discovery in the crypt has opened up an even wider fissure at Sandchester's cathedral than that which the building work was intended to rectify. It is believed that the divisions amongst dean and chapter are wider now than at any time since the Reformation, due in no small part to the discovery of bones believed by many to be those of Saint Aldwould.*
>
> *A campaign has already begun to reconstruct the lost shrine of Sandchester's forgotten saint and to restore the cathedral to its pre-reformation beauty. It is hardly necessary to add that there are just as many opponents of the scheme, who would prefer the plain, whitewashed walls to be left as they are.*
>
> *Neither Dean Watts nor Dr Brinkwater, the chancellor, who are widely regarded as leading lights of their respective factions, have yet commented on either the find, or the restoration."*

I returned the cuttings to their envelope and looked to Holmes for his comments. He was deep in thought and remained silent for several minutes.

At length he stood and reached for our 'Bradshaw'. As he flicked through the pages he addressed me, absently, as though still deep in thought about the case: "If you can be packed in half an hour, Watson, there is an excellent dining express for Sandchester at eleven. I suspect this case may have more to offer us than architectural curiosities and old bones but since neither the newspapers nor Miss Watts have enlightened us, we really must sample the delights of the 'Pilgrim's Rest' and find out for ourselves!"

A telegram from Charing Cross ensured that we were met at Sandchester station by Dean Watts's groom, with a dog cart. We were whisked immediately to the Deanery, while our luggage sped on its way to our hotel. Miss Watts, a slight but determined woman of about five and twenty, greeted us effusively and escorted us immediately to her father's study.

The Dean, the Very Reverend Lancelot Watts, was clearly a man broken in health and careworn almost unto death. He sat in a deep winged chair, bolstered with cushions, looking for all the world as though he had fallen into it from a great height. Nonetheless, he craned forward as we arrived and though he addressed us in a faltering, cracked voice; his eyes were bright and keen.

"Thank heaven you have come gentlemen" he began, "this business is almost too much for a frame weakened by illness and controversy. I have held them at bay these five years but I cannot do so much longer. My daughter at first thought me misguided in seeking outside aid but I knew, I *knew* you would come to save us. You are aware of the Sandchester dispute, I presume?"

"No, sir" replied Holmes. "Is it relevant?"

The Dean chuckled. "You are right Mr Holmes. I must not waste your time. However, the 'dispute' as the *Ecclesiologist* termed it when it first reached the publc eye in the spring of '88, is at the heart of this affair. In short, Mr Holmes, the cathedral here is bitterly divided. Half the Chapter would have us rebuild and redecorate as though

Henry VIII had never split with Rome, while the rest of us believe in The Word and in whitewash."

"To be candid Mr Holmes, I feel certain that until a fortnight ago my 'High Church' foes were content to wait until my death. Then, they would have every reason to expect the Chancellor, Dr Brinkwater, to succeed me and carry out their scheme of 'beautification'. Now, with the collapse in the crypt and the discovery of the bones, they will brook no delay and we 'Low Churchmen' are laid low indeed."

"You believe then that the bones are those of Saint Aldwould?" I asked.

"Oh no, my dear Dr Watson, the bones are those of Dr Brinkwater!"

****

The Dean was gripped then by some form of seizure. A glass of brandy seemed to settle him and it was agreed that while he rested, we should continue our investigation in the crypt. Miss Watts would conclude the Dean's story as we walked through the Close and cathedral to the stair beside the great stone screen that divided nave from choir.

As the cathedral clock struck four, we stood before the newly revealed chantry. It was little more than a small, stone booth; providing space for a stone plinth, or tomb chest, which contained a stone coffin. The coffin had been covered with a slab of dark marble bearing the indent of a long-gone brass effigy but that slab now lay propped against the tomb chest. At the east end of the diminutive private chapel was a desk-like stone altar. To our left, roped off, was a large and untidy pile of masonry. To our right stood the cathedral clerk of works, a Mr Garfoot, and the Sandchester Constabulary's senior detective, Chief Inspector Balsam.

"Well, Miss Watts, er...gentlemen" began Garfoot, set in motion by a nudge from the chief inspector, "you see before you a typical, if rather modest, chantry chapel of about 1450. The brass, though now gone, was that of a priest with mitre and bishop's staff. The carved arms around the door suggest that it may have been prepared to house the bones of Bishop Akehurst, who was promoted to the..."

"I suspect these gentlemen are more interested in more recent developments" interrupted Chief Inspector Balsam in a voice which combined the local accent with signs of a heavy cold. "The damp hereabouts is getting into *my* bones and I see no reason to prolong our visit."

"Yes, well..." continued Garfoot, "as far as I can tell, the chapel was walled up behind what was, in effect, an internal buttress some time in the 1670s, when the short spire was added to the central tower of the cathedral. I daresay they felt at the time that the extra weight might threaten the walls above us in the crossing and nave."

"I was thinking of developments this month" interrupted Balsam again with a sniff.

"Ah" continued the clerk of works imperturbably. "Well, yes, gentlemen and...er...Miss Watts, yes. Well, a fortnight ago it was pointed out to me that a large, wide, crack had developed in the 'buttress' and since it has long been a contention of mine that the spire is actually no threat to the cathedral's fabric and that the 'buttress' therefore serves no purpose, I proposed that we remove it. The buttress that is...not the crack."

"Quite so" added Holmes with a smile, "what do you suppose caused the crack?"

"Ah well, that *is* interesting," responded Garfoot, undismayed by a sharp intake of breath from the chief inspector. "I couldn't explain it and even Dr Staveley seemed unsure..."

"Dr Staveley?" asked Holmes.

"Oh, yes. Dr Staveley is the Headmaster of the Cathedral School...and Residentiary Canon of course. He has devoted a lifetime to the place and really knows more of its ins and outs than anyone else. A truly learned man, Dr Staveley. He is our archivist and has been Treasurer, sacrist and even acted as precentor for a year while Dr Evans was in South Africa..."

"But he couldn't explain the crack" interrupted the chief inspector again.

"Er...no" replied Garfoot quietly. "So, we poked about in the crack and down came the whole lot of stonework. We found this little chantry chapel hidden underneath."

"With the bones laid in the stone coffin?" I asked.

"Yes, sir. Well, not bones really. Or not *just* bones if you understand me." Garfoot shot a nervous glance at Miss Watts before he continued. "More skin and bones really."

The chef inspector here stepped half a pace forward, leaning an arm on the half-blocked window ledge of the chantry chapel. He gestured with a tilt of his head, deeply buried in his coat collar, towards the interior of the chapel.

"We found Dr Brinkwater inside. Head stove in. And not by accident either. He'd been dead, we reckoned, about four weeks. Maybe less. He had been seen to leave for a little holiday up at his old college in Oxford a month ago. He'd sent his bags on ahead to the station. They reached Oxford but he didn't. I suppose he himself didn't get further than the crypt, which isn't really on the way to Oxford...if you take my meaning."

"Indeed" replied Holmes.

"I don't follow" said I. "How did Dr Brinkwater get inside the chapel, if it was still buried by the masonry?"

"Good question" replied the chief inspector. "Mr Garfoot here says the crack was just about big enough but..."

"Yes?" asked Holmes.

"Well, Mr Holmes, the crack didn't appear until ten days or so after Dr Brinkwater had left for (but not arrived in) Oxford."

****

With Miss Watts feeling faint and the chief inspector complaining ever more plaintively about the cold, damp air of the crypt, we returned to the cathedral close and thence to our lodgings. Balsam accompanied us on the promise of a reviving drink. Once established in a corner of the Pilgrim's Rest's saloon bar, the policeman became more confiding.

"I understand you were summoned by the Dean" he began. "A nice old gentleman and well liked, even if he has to be pushed along a bit by Dr Staveley sometimes. But Mr Holmes, I should warn you that were you to ask me who benefitted most by this death; I'd have to say it was Dr Watts himself. This row in the chapter he spoke of – well, it has divided the cathedral and half of Sandchester this last twelvemonth. It is a bitter business, gentlemen. As bitter as my beer," at which the chief inspector drank deeply from his tankard, setting it heavily down upon the table.

"I tell you, I was glad to keep them all at bay with the speculation about holy relics. If they knew whose bones really was a-mould'ring in the grave down there, I'd get no peace for my investigations. None at all."

The chief inspector drained his tankard and wiped his moustache with the back of his hand. He wished us a good evening but paused beside our table and bent low to deliver his parting shot.

"To be frank with you gentlemen, if the Dean were not at death's door, so to speak, I think I might have had to take him into custody already. I tell you, it is not a pretty business."

The chief inspector left us and I began to study the brief menu, fixed in a frame on the wall of the bar.

"You're not eager for too early a dinner, I trust, Watson?" asked my friend.

"Not at all, if you have something in mind" I replied with some resignation.

"Come then Watson, we have work to do."

With increasing incredulity I followed Holmes back to the Close and through a side door into the deserted cathedral. To my surprise Holmes produced a lantern, lighting our way back to the crypt and the pile of stone beside the tiny chantry chapel.

"Hold this," commanded my friend, handing me the lantern, while he proceeded to clamber amongst the stones. For half an hour he tore at the pile of masonry; pulling up large stone blocks, examining them and then dashing them down again with an expression of frustration or dissatisfaction.

"What are you looking for, Holmes?" I asked.

"For the mouldings from around a door," he replied, "if some form of entry to the chapel was concealed within the buttress, its lintel or frame should still be evident amongst these fragments."

At length Holmes slid down from the rock-pile, shaking his head in frustration and dusting off his coat and trousers. He beckoned me to follow and strode to the chantry chapel. Once again, he began a close examination of the area, slapping at the close fitting ashlar walls and probing the few cracks and crevices with his fingers.

Then, he entered the chapel itself. Once again his fingers ran across the carved decorations and an inscription which ran across the stone behind the tiny altar. Holmes bent low, grunting as he pressed hard against the walls on every side. Finally, he put his weight and strength against the tomb itself; the low stone coffin in which had been found the remains of Dr Brinkwater.

With a sudden, sharp cry (though whether of effort, surprise, or triumph I could not tell) my friend simply vanished! The low stone, barely two feet square, which formed the eastern end of the tomb chest upon which the coffin rested, had given way and fallen inwards, carrying Holmes with it.

I hastened into the chantry and knelt with my back to the altar, gazing into the inky blackness into which Holmes had disappeared.

"Holmes! Holmes!" I cried but there was no answer. In vain I held the lantern to the square hole. I lit a match and threw it down into the hole but it sputtered immediately and went out. I found a ha'penny in my pocket and tossed it after the match. This time I could gauge the drop at something around ten feet, as the coin sang and bounced in the darkness.

I called for my friend again to no effect. Then I realised that I must find help – and quickly. He was clearly unconscious and possibly badly hurt too.

I ran as fast as the dim light of Holmes's lantern would permit. I emerged into the crossing beneath the tower and re-entered the nave beside the stone screen. I ran along the north aisle, my lantern sending striking shadows across my path from the pillars and funerary monuments which loomed up from the darkness on either side.

The main west door was locked and barred. I turned to my right and by a miracle found a small, low door which yielded to my shoulder and opened onto an area of lawn beside one of the magnificent flying buttresses of the western porch. I staggered into the cool night air and looked about me to find the Dean's house, where I would at least find help and a ladder or rope.

Instead a hand restrained me.

"Steady! Watson. Let us pause before we act!"

"Holmes!" I cried. "Holmes…you are all right. I called but heard no answer."

"I'm sorry Watson. I was winded by my fall and by the time you called again, I had wandered too far from the entrance of the vault into which I fell."

"A vault?"

"Oh yes Watson. I knew there must be some way into the chantry, even while it was buried inside the buttress. We are wading in murky waters and must tread carefully."

"You know more of this then than I have seen. I believe Holmes that you know who is behind Dr Brinkwater's death."

"Dr Brinkwater's *murder*, Watson. Let us not forget that. We are up against a subtle villain, who has gambled for high stakes and has not yet given up his hopes of winning all."

"But who is it, Holmes?" I asked, "surely not Dr Watts?"

"No, Watson, not the Dean."

"Not Miss Watts?"

"No, Watson. Dr Staveley is our prey. Remember Watson, it is Staveley who knows this place like the back of his hand. It is Staveley who will gain from the removal not only of his principal High Church opponent but also the poor, sick Dean. As Dean Watts's closest supporter, Dr Staveley would have every hope of succeeding him. It is Staveley, Watson, who has held every office but the highest the cathedral can offer."

Holmes brushed himself down, sweeping a cloud of dust and cobwebs to the ground.

"Despite appearances, my dear fellow, I was following a well worn path. Beneath the little chantry is a wider burial vault. It is reached by a passage-way which winds its way through the foundations of the nave. It is a tight squeeze but wide enough to permit a coffin to pass. It may be forgotten by Mr Garfoot and his staff but someone has been back and forth along it many times in the last few months; of that I am sure. Who more likely than Staveley; that delver into every corner of the cathedral's past? Who more likely to find an ancient, forgotten reference to such a secret thoroughfare than the cathedral's sometime archivist?"

"We must hurry to find Chief Inspector Balsam" I declared.

"Not so fast, Watson. How can we prove our allegation? We have a chain of reasoning, and a motive but not a grain of proof. Without that we cannot act."

"But Holmes," I replied, "surely Balsam could search Staveley's lodgings. That might turn up some evidence."
"Indeed it might but we shall have difficulty convincing Balsam to take such a step and even allowing that we could and that he agreed to a search, where would our case be if we found nothing?"

****

Midnight found us in the burial vault beneath the newly discovered chantry chapel. While I alerted Mr Garfoot and the Chief Inspector, Holmes had written a short note to Dr Staveley informing him that, at ten next morning, it was the intention of the authorities to break into the chantry chapel's tomb in search of the bones of St. Aldwould.

"I told him that the Dean was determined to scotch rumours of Holy relics once and for all," explained Holmes, "and that he might wish to be present out of antiquarian interest. Such an operation would clearly alarm Staveley. What if we accidentally broke into his hidden vault? No, I think we might reasonably expect that Dr Staveley would prefer to spend the night before sealing up the 'chute' which precipitated me from the tomb chest to the burial vault below and up which he climbed to hide Dr Brinkwater's body a few weeks ago."

Never have I spent a more miserable night. I sat on a velvet-covered coffin with Garfoot, while Holmes and Baslam occupied a niche beside the entrance. We remained in utter darkness and nearly complete silence, while my limbs cried out for relief from inaction in the cold, damp night air. Twice Balsam suppressed a sneeze and at about three o'clock a sudden gulp or snore from Garfoot told me that he had succumbed to sleep. I was glad to have the excuse to exercise my elbow.

As the first light of reluctant dawn crept into the crypt and filtered down into our hiding place, we realised that the game was up. Either Holmes was wrong and Staveley knew nothing of the vault, or he had somehow scented our trap.

"Well, gentlemen," remarked Holmes, his voice betraying no sign of disappointment or our nocturnal ordeal, "we have failed this time. We must return to the Cathedral Close and rally our forces over the Dean's breakfast table."

Our council of war however proved stillborn. The deanery was in turmoil and the poor dean prostrate. The Dean's daughter, Miss Watts, and Dr Staveley had fled Sandchester. They were traced to the railway station and to the first train of the morning for London. Thereafter, no trace was found either by Scotland Yard or Chief Inspector Balsam's force.

"Well, well, Watson," remarked Sherlock Holmes, as we travelled by the same route that afternoon, "we have been well and truly bested this time. There was clearly iron in that young lady's soul and I fancy she was the source of much of the Dean's resistance to the opposing faction. No wonder she opposed her father's plan to write to me. It is a moot point whether the Miss Watts was a willing accomplice of

Staveley's or a trustingly innocent companion. Doubtless the police will find her soon enough if it is the latter and if the former, she may yet cross our path again, Watson!"

"For now I advise you to file the case under 'F' for failure and urge you to publish it, with the others you find there, as an antidote to my own conceit and the folly of those who imagine that I invariably succeed and can achieve the impossible!"

The Affair of the Silver Bandsman

Contemplating the many cases in which I had the privilege of observing Mr Sherlock Holmes at work, I am often struck by the singular fact that he was seldom, if ever, entirely at leisure. In truth, I have often seen him exhausted, prostrate, at the conclusion of a case yet a few hours sleep or a good meal, from our admirable housekeeper, almost invariably served to restore my friend to a state of keen anticipation of his next challenge.

Occasionally, the absence of work would frustrate and infuriate Sherlock Holmes but in most cases he simply threw himself into some other form of investigation or endeavour. For days on end he would paste newspaper cuttings or photographs into his scrapbooks or files, or smoke his way through dozens of exotic cigars, to categorise and record their appearance, feel, scent and ash.

Crime was by no means his sole occupation. Like any professional, Sherlock Holmes often sought diversion from his work as an aid to it. His music, for example, served to free his mind from cerebral dead-ends and open new pathways for thought. The notion of a holiday - sight-seeing, walking or golfing - would hardly have appealed to Holmes but on one or two occasions I recollect trips for his health's sake or to further the research which absorbed him at that time.

One such excursion occurred soon after a melancholy interlude in my own life, which had resulted in my brief return to Baker Street and abandonment, for several months, of my practice. Holmes, I suspect having taken notice of my own low spirits, suddenly announced that a holiday would do us good and that he was determined upon a short sojourn in the Midlands, where he could best further some research into a batch of Mercian charters, which he held to be medieval forgeries.

Within a few short hours, a stopping train from St Pancras delivered us to a near-deserted halt, from whence we travelled two or three miles through heavy-clayed fields, much hedged and copsed, to the sprawling hill-top village of Bredon Priors.

As we swayed to and fro in the station fly, Holmes discoursed on the landscape and history of the area. "The very name of the place," he observed, "tells us much of its past. 'Bre-don' itself is derived from two ancient British words meaning a hill settlement, the 'Priors' denotes its later ownership by a Priory. In this case that of Mettleham, where I believe the charters I have been studying were forged."

Our conveyance jolted us suddenly as we turned into a narrower lane which led through a thick copse or grove of trees. "Ah, this is indeed the true hunting country, Watson. These copses are ideal breeding ground for foxes and, with the hedges and ditches round about, I fancy are carefully maintained to keep Reynard and his family in fine chase-able fettle."

He pointed with his stick, sweeping it across the landscape. "These fields were once open and ploughed in rotation but from the eighteenth century have been cut into the familiar patchwork which now seems so English. Underneath you can still see the ridges and furrows of ancient ploughing. The original fields and boundaries which I hope to trace, in my pursuit of our forgers of charters!"

Within a few minutes we had arrived at our destination, and a smiling landlord was welcoming us to the seemingly charming inn, which was to be our home for the next week at least.

"I am delighted to see you gentlemen. I have two excellent bed-chambers and an adjoining sitting room, with a fire laid and dinner in two hours' time; just as your letter stated."

Our host here hesitated and his beaming countenance briefly clouded over.

"I regret," he added, "that I cannot guarantee the peace and quiet and 'studious atmosphere' of which your letter also spoke."

"Oh?" Asked Holmes with a slight smile and that sudden alertness or hint of excited anticipation I had come to recognise as typical of the start of so many of his adventures. "Why so, my dear fellow, what can have happened to mar the tranquillity of so delightful and peaceful a spot?"

Our host's head fell upon his chest in embarrassment. "I'm afraid it is largely my doing gentlemen. My excitement at having such renowned guests got the better of me and I must have told a few of my regulars in the bar here, when first I received your letter. The word has gone round and already half the parish is dreaming up family mysteries for you to solve."

"Oh really!" I declared, rather more warmly than I intended, "this won't do. Mr Holmes is here for a rest and to study..." but Holmes held up a hand as though to waft away the annoyance.

"My dear Watson, what harm can it do? How often has a really quite worthy puzzle come our way from an apparently uninspiring source? Remember that business of the Copper Beeches? Or the affair of Hilton Cubitt's coded messages?"

He turned to our landlord. "Let them come. We may find these tales beguiling and are under no obligation, in any case, to act."

We had turned away to see our luggage carried safely into the inn, when a dog cart clattered into the courtyard and came to sudden halt in a spray of gravel and dust. From it tumbled the very image of a country physician, in a cut-away coat and tall hat of a style worn several seasons ago in the

City. The new arrival ignored us and addressed himself urgently to our host.

"We'll need your parlour Harry. There's been a peculiar death at the works and Inspector Harris wants the corpse laid out for the coroner. The body's coming on the works' ambulance and the coroner's been telegraphed for from Leicester. Harris is on the warpath, so don't make trouble, there's a good chap."

"A *peculiar* death! How very gratifying", murmured my friend, although he made no attempt to question the doctor. Within a few more minutes a short, stoutish, red-faced man in a tight tweed suit and low-crowned bowler marched into the yard. The newcomer's sharp eyes took in the whole inn yard at a glance and he strode over to the doctor's trap; obviously searching for a sign of its owner.

The doctor then emerged from the inn and greeted the newcomer with a cheery "Well met Inspector. To the band hall is it?"

This was acknowledged with a nod from the red-faced fellow, who leaped aboard the cart with surprising agility. He flicked the horse with the reins and we now found ourselves across the turning-circle of the dog-cart.

"Stand back there" ordered the inspector sharply, his outstretched arm across my friend's chest. "This is police business and we can't have 'gawpers' impeding investigations."

"This is Mr Sherlock Holmes", I responded angrily, "and many of your superiors at Scotland Yard have been pleased to have his assistance in cases of unexplained death."

The inspector turned a pair of sharp eyes upon me, his reddish side-whiskers bristling. "What makes you think this is unexplained? And what makes you think we of the local constabulary require assistance?"

"Quite right inspector," purred my friend quietly. "Quite right. But to interrupt your well-earned game of billiards, after being already on duty all night-long, this case must be *somewhat* out of the ordinary. What harm can sharing the little you already know do?"

The inspector turned his eyes to Holmes and stroked his chin. After a moment or two he smiled and nodded his agreement.

"Mr Sherlock Holmes...yes, the name does mean something to me. Something of your methods and achievements has reached us, even out here in the shires."

The inspector nodded his head in thought. Then he brushed a white dust from his left sleeve. "Now, let me see", he said, "there's the chalk from my billiards – that's easy enough. As for the all-night duty...that is my stubble, I'm thinking, and right enough again. Even down here we are expected to turn out shaved but we had a rick fire last night and I've been over at Larkington 'til after breakfast and so didn't get back to the station until it was too late to nip home."

The police inspector again rubbed the back of his thumb across his chin and nodded at Sherlock Holmes. "You gentlemen would have come up on the 4.15 stopper I'm thinking. Drove up here on the station fly but took the long way up the hill, rather than the direct but steeper lane past Capell's Farm."

"Ha!" roared my friend. "We have a fellow practitioner here, Watson! A knowledge of timetables and of where the puddles are to be found on every country lane! Capital! But will he allow us in on the case?"

The inspector's grim visage cracked into a smile. "He will, Mr Holmes and happy to do so – but I fear it is likely to be of no great interest." Here the inspector gestured towards the vacant seats of the cart. "We have a poor fellow seems to have dropped dead while playing with the Silver Band and though there's always rivalry in the band, none of 'em are really the cut-throat type. I'd be surprised if it turns out to be more than heart failure or apoplexy."

"Please come and have a look though," he said and with a nod to me, added: "and a second opinion from a medical man will be welcome too, if Dr Draycott doesn't object."

A few minutes sufficed to bring us to the gates of the Bredon Priors Mineral-Water and Ginger Beer Company's works. There, another constable and two or three workers awaited us beside the band hall; a long, single-storied brick building, which adjoined the stables and sheds of the factory. From the hall came the unmistakeable sounds of 'Men of Harlech'; though after a minute or two, the music gave way to shouting, mixed with laughter.

Inspector Harris led us into the hall, where we found arrayed in front of us the Bredon Silver Band – seemingly undismayed at the loss of one of its members.

"Where is he?" asked the inspector, addressing the conductor, who stood with baton raised beside a large wooden music stand.

"Through there," replied the conductor, with a slight nod of the head towards a doorway, across which someone had drawn a faded reddish curtain.

Behind the curtain was a surprisingly large and well-equipped kitchen, with a small range, a sink, and an extensive array of plates, dishes and mugs. The body of a short, square-shouldered man lay across three folding, wooden chairs.

With Dr Draycott I examined the body. It took only a few minutes to reach our conclusion and I took Holmes to one side while Draycott spoke to the inspector.

"It doesn't look to me like heart failure or apoplexy," I observed soberly, "Dr Draycott and I are entirely in agreement that we seem to have here a case of poisoning; though quite what poison and how administered we are unsure. The smell around this man's lips and nose and the discolouration in the same area are quite distinctive. To be candid, if it were not clearly impossible (given that the poor fellow collapsed whilst playing) Dr. Draycott and I agree that we would diagnose gas-poisoning!"

At that moment the curtain behind us was drawn violently to one side and the conductor, closely followed by a tall, heavily bearded man, entered the kitchen.

"I hope you will excuse our continuing the practice," muttered the conductor. "We have a contest on Saturday and I've no doubt Jethro wouldn't have wanted us to falter just a-cause he's snuffed it."

"What's this?" demanded Inspector Harris. "Constable! Find Sergeant Jessop, tell him I want a man on this door – er- curtain here, and you start taking names and statements from the bandsmen. I want to know every man who was here when *Jethro* here died."

Harris turned again to the conductor. "I am Inspector Harris of the county police. This here is Mr Sherlock Holmes, who may also ask you questions about this affair. So, who are you and what do you know of the death?"

"Ah, well," replied the conductor, "my name is Bowden; Godfrey Bowden, and I am the bandmaster of the Bredon Silver Band. This gentleman, with me, is Edgar Brinsley. He is our band secretary. The dead man, there, is...er...was Jethro Tolliver; our principal euphonium."

"Yes," nodded Brinsley from behind the conductor's shoulder, "and without our first euph' goodness knows how we'll do tomorrow."

"We'll do what I always said we should do," snarled Bowden in reply, "and give the 'solo' back to Wally Raikes. If you lot weren't in mortal fear of Tolliver, he'd never have had it in the first place!"

Inspector Harris proceeded to tease out from Bowden, with occasional hissed interjections from the band secretary, the events surrounding Jethro Tolliver's death.

Later that evening, as we sat smoking in our small sitting room at the inn, Holmes gently dissected the evidence we had heard. The band had assembled for the first of two extended practices before an important contest. The band's key piece featured a solo for cornet but almost at the last minute, Tolliver had insisted that he alone had the talent and tone to carry it off and had bullied the band into agreeing that the part be switched from cornet to euphonium.

Shortly after the start of the final practice, that morning, Tolliver had been seized with a fit of coughing. The euphonium fell from his grasp and before the astonished bandsmen; he had slumped from his chair and fallen insensible to the floor. Before anyone could loosen his collar or proffer a glass of water, Tolliver was dead.

"You diagnosed poison, Watson," remarked Holmes, tapping the ash from his cigar. "That indicates murder. Who are our suspects and what are their motives?"

"Clearly," I replied, "there was little love lost between Brinsley and Tolliver and I imagine this Wally Raikes wasn't best pleased to lose his solo."

"Yes, Watson," agreed Sherlock Holmes. "These makers of music seem very discordant in their relationships. What, though, was the hold Tolliver had over the band, and how did he impose his will with such ease?"

Our host had just entered the room to clear away our dinner plates and glasses and, hearing Holmes's question, he interrupted us:

"I beg your pardon gentlemen," said our host quietly, "I think I can help you there. You see, everything with that band begins and ends with the Mineral water and Ginger Beer factory. It is 'fizzy-pop' that houses the band and 'pop' that pays for the instruments and the uniforms. And Tolliver is, that is *was*, old Mr Bainbrigge's son-in-law. That and manager at the place too."

"Old Bainbrigge?" I asked.

"Silas Bainbrigge set up the works some thirty years ago to exploit an old spring on the hillside west of the village. He won the contract for the whole of the railway, Midland and Joints, about ten years after that and never looked back. They say even Lord Salisbury quaffs Bredon Priors' mineral water and every other passenger between London, Manchester and Sheffield washes down his Pullman dinner with it. Half the ginger beer in the Midlands comes from Bredon Priors and on top of that there's lemonade, soda water, and goodness knows what else besides. Anyway, Bainbrigge gives Tolliver the running of the works and if he don't like your face, you're out! Of works and works' band both."

The picture our host painted was of a band dominated by a malign bully, aided and abetted by a neglectful employer, and with a coterie of spineless and sycophantic hangers-on, whose support earned them promotion at work.

"Any of them could be the murderer!" I declared, "and I scarcely blame them."

"Indeed, Watson, but one of them translated justifiable resentment into brutal action. We must see what the post-mortem examination produces and see who had the genius to administer a mysterious poison, in plain view of a band practice! We have a worthy foeman here, Watson. But for our interest perhaps, or a less capable detective or scrupulous doctor, they would be burying Tolliver as the simple victim of a seizure."

Our breakfast the following morning was scarcely completed when Inspector Harris burst in upon us.

"Gentlemen," he declared, "it is poison! Moreover, it is a compound only slightly changed from the very gas that is both generated by and used in the processes which create

Bredon Priors mineral waters and temperance beers. I have my eye on Godfrey Bowden, thwarted band master and chief chemist at the factory, but frankly, if I can't explain how poison gas could be administered in plain view of an entire band, the coroner's jury will surely put it down to a delayed effect of an accidental inhalation at work."

"Indeed?" responded Holmes. "You may very well be right, Inspector, but I think (with your indulgence) that I should like a look at Tolliver's euphonium before I came to any conclusion."

"By all means," replied Harris indulgently. "I'll join you later, but I have already tested the mouthpiece without finding a trace of poison and there is nothing else to see."

An hour later Holmes and I were once again in the band hall, waiting for Edgar Brinsley to produce the euphonium.

"You clearly do not fall in with the inspector's reading of the case," I suggested.

My friend gave me a sideways look, full of amused mischief.

"I have two objections to the inspector's hypothesis," replied Sherlock Holmes. "The first is that while Bowden may have both motive and ability, he seems, to me, entirely to lack the ruthlessness such a scheme would require. My second is simply that if Harris is right, there is nothing more to be done and we should have to return to our charters. That I cannot contemplate."

The door opened before I could reply and Brinsley placed the euphonium into Holmes's hands. The examination which followed lasted fully ten minutes, as my friend unscrewed every valve and piston, opening each drain and tuning slide; sniffing at them in turn. He turned the instrument slowly over in his hands, carefully catching the few drops of trapped moisture in a saucer. Finally, Holmes stared into the bell of the euphonium.

Suddenly, he presented the mouth of the bell to Brinsley, thrusting it to within a few inches of his face.

"How do you account for those scratches? They are clear signs of repeated, vigorous probing, scratching or poking, deep into the instrument over many months if not years!"

Brinsley's mouth curled in a grimace of disgust. "Indeed they are Mr Holmes. Years of it. Yet another instance of Tolliver's humiliation of his rivals. Hardly a practice went by without his seizing the conductor's baton, to poke and scrape away at his instrument. You see, Tolliver was a chewer of tobacco and despite frequent distasteful shifting of his quids, the dribble of the man was forever getting inside and clogging-up the instrument. Truly, he was a monster. How Bowden could meekly take back the baton, sticky with tobacco juice, I cannot imagine."

Holmes placed the euphonium carefully upon a table, moving a pile of band parts and music books to make room. He turned once again to the band secretary.

"Where are the instruments kept? When not being played by the band."

Edgar Brinsley swallowed loudly. "Most...the cornets, tenors and flugelhorns are taken home by their players; theoretically so that they can practice their parts. The larger instruments, including that euphonium is usually locked away in the band store and brought out for practices."

" 'Locked away' you say?" I asked. "Who then has the keys?"

"I have a set. Mr Bowden has one. Charles Rush (our principal bass player keeps one, so that he can call section practices at will, and I believe Wally Raikes also has a set of keys, as he keeps the place clean and tidy."

At this moment the door opened to permit Inspector Harris to enter the band room. My friend Sherlock Holmes smiled broadly in greeting before turning again to the band secretary. "This Wally Raikes; where is he employed in the ginger beer works?"

"Wally? He is in charge of the gas plant – heating and lighting – but he is a regular jack of all trades; inventing a new bottle top one day and a new flavouring for pop the next. There seems nothing he won't turn his hand to."

"Tell me," asked Sherlock Holmes, "has this Wally Raikes done any experimental work with gelatine lately, or thin animal skins?"

"Thin animals?" queried Brinsley.

"The skins," replied Holmes with a sigh, "not the animals. Sausage skins, intestines, and the like?"

"Er…I think there was some question of using that sort of thing in sealing jars but really I am hardly the best placed to know…"

Holmes clapped his hands together. "Ha! I think we have him. Inspector, I suggest we saw open this euphonium."

"Saw it open?!" expostulated the band secretary, "but that is a Boosey 'Sonorous' brand euphonium and, although it is somewhat soiled, there are a good many more years of first section competitive playing left in it."

"I think we'll saw it open then" replied Inspector Harris, who seemed somehow to have fallen into Holmes's way of thinking – though as yet I remained in the dark.

"Let me fetch Wally and his tools. Perhaps we can break it apart at the seams and hope to re-solder later?"

"An excellent idea," agreed Holmes. "It would be a shame to destroy so valuable an instrument and Mr Raikes's presence might, in any case, be helpful."

Inspector Harris nodded to a policeman and within a few minutes Raikes, his face a mixture of apprehension and curiosity, joined us. Harris handed him the euphonium.

"Break it open would you?" the police detective asked quietly. "Here, please, where the bell is fitted into the 'U' shape. Do you follow me, so we can see what is going on just down there out of sight?"

Raikes snatched the instrument from him, his face contorted with rage. "I'll do no such thing. Damn me if I do. Why? It would ruin a fine euphonium."

Inspector Harris frowned darkly. "Now then, if you won't do it, I'll have Constable Coffin here crack it open and if he does it, there'll assuredly be no mending her."

"I won't do it!"

"Permit me," said Holmes stretching forward to take up both the euphonium and Raikes's bag of tools. With surprising skill, my friend levered apart the instrument. For a moment he peered into the stomach of the thing. Then, with the tip of his silver pencil, he drew from the tobacco-darkened edges of the newly bared metal, a thin, opaque film which shone, iridescent, in the bright sunlight.

The inspector broke our trance. "Take him!" he roared, pointing at Raikes. The small, red faced man wriggled and spat but Constable Coffin was more than a match for the solo cornet player.

"But what does this mean?" I gasped.

"It means murder," responded Inspector Harris quietly, "and a more cunning affair I have yet to see. I take my hat off to you Mr Holmes, I really do. How you saw through such a plot I cannot begin to guess."

"What plot?" I exploded. "How on earth did Raikes kill a man with gas in the company of a whole band, from a seat yards away?"

Sherlock Holmes lit a cigarette, tossing the match towards the door of the band room. "There, Watson, you have the genius of the plan. Raikes's motive is clear enough. The ogre Tolliver was destroying the band and making life miserable for all around him. Those little touches of vindictive spite – scraping out tobacco juice from the euphonium with the bandmaster's baton – simply brought home Tolliver's dominance and rubbed salt into wounds which were already raw."

Holmes turned to Raikes, now slumped against the constable; more supported than restrained by him.

"I fancy, the idea of murder had been in your mind some time, Wally Raikes. Was it the loss of the solo part which finally goaded you into action?"

Raikes eyed Holmes for a few moments and then nodded weakly. "Aye. It was the solo that did it. That and the arrival of the new gelatine substitute. Amazing stuff; a by-product of explosives but so malleable. I hoped to use it, stretched, to seal jars of a new line of preserves or jelly. I thought I might be able to thin it out further and tried bubbling a number of gases from the works through it. It didn't work but one evening, when I was alone in the laboratory, I managed to get it to form great bubbles of the gas, which bounced about the room."

"It amused me at the time but that night I suddenly had the idea that a sack, or bubble of the poisonous gas could be forced into the euphonium. Tolliver would blow away and eventually get nothing out of the other end. He'd be bound to think it was his stinking tobacco spit and to poke at the bell. Well, that would be perfect. The bubble of poison gas would be burst by the baton and he'd get a face-full of it. At the very least it'd make him sick and teach him a lesson. With luck it'd be the end of him."

"Ah, now," interrupted the Inspector. "If that was the way of it, it is high time I cautioned you. What you say will be taken down and *will* be used against you. I am a fair man and I'll not take advantage of you."

Raikes nodded again, his head hanging lower still towards his chest. My friend, Sherlock Holmes stood and brushed a residue of cigarette ash from his waistcoat.

"Our work, my dear Inspector Harris, is done. This case is in good hands. Watson and I must return to our Anglo-Saxon charters and crimes of an entirely different age."

The Affair of the Missing Passenger

Although generally fastidious in his personal habits and dress, my friend Sherlock Holmes, could also be sufficiently single-minded in the pursuit of whatever project preoccupied him, as to abandon (temporarily) his conventional tidiness or habit of civilised conduct. This often led to a dramatic break-through in a case; it could also lead to a break-down in relations with his long-suffering landlady-cum-housekeeper, Mrs Hudson.

I very well recollect returning to Baker Street one blustery afternoon in the autumn of 1890; shortly after the affair of the red headed men. Outside, London was a whirl of falling leaves and bustling traffic, with such gusts of wind between buildings that I hastened along the Marylebone Road with one hand firmly upon the brim of my hat for fear of losing it.

It was a considerable relief therefore to reach the familiar door of number 221B. One glance at the alarm on Mrs Hudson's welcoming face however dashed my hopes of finding a haven of peace within. Indeed, as I ascended the stairs (silently counting to myself each tread as I passed) I sensed a domestic maelstrom within our old shared rooms.

My trepidation was not justified however. Certainly the old sitting room was a veritable snowstorm of newspapers and my old friend knelt, inches deep in them but my overall impression was one of excitement rather than of anger or frustration.

"Ah! Watson" cried my old friend with palpable relief. "At last! My dear Watson, save my sanity, please! My 'M' is vanished…lost; half the file quite gone…"
"M for missing, eh?" I replied.
"M for misplaced, I fear" nodded Holmes with a shadow of a smile.

"Well," I mused, hesitantly, "you know my methods; apply them!"

Holmes smiled again, broadly this time. "Watson, you are a tonic." He swept an assortment of news-clippings from our best armchair and urged me to sit. "Where have you been these past few weeks? That little skirmish with John Clay surely cannot have exhausted you so much?"

"Not at all" I replied gravely. "I have been busy with my practice but to be candid, I am more preoccupied with Mary. I am afraid my dear wife has not been well. You know how they speak of doctor's wives? Well, there is some truth in the saying it seems and I have despatched Mary, at last, to the south coast to stay with friends until her throat is better."

Holmes's face assumed a grave expression as he surveyed mine.

"It is nothing, I assure you," I responded. "If it were anything more than an over persistent cough, I should hardly have left her side."

My friend nodded again but remained thoughtful.

I broke the silence. "This volume of Ms then? Musgrave? Milverton? Some of your best cases. When did you last have it?"

Holmes stroked his long chin thoughtfully. "Oh, indeed Watson, that file has been in almost constant use of late. M is a singularly haunted letter. You'll remember the unfortunate Melas and of course (as you know better than I) there is Morstan. Of late, I have begun to accumulate another 'M' too. Quite a rising star of crime in our metropolis."

I should have liked to have dug deeper into this new villain of the alaphabet but at that moment we were interrupted by a tap at the door and the entry of Mrs Hudson with a tray of tea and cake.

In a moment Holmes swept yet another pile of papers from the table, offering the newly freed surface to Mrs Hudson with a gesture of the hand.

A sharp intake of breath made clear that stern lady's displeasure, as her eyes took in the drifts of newsprint which rustled beneath her skirts.

"I have misplaced most of 'M'", explained Holmes, with a surprisingly meek tone.

"M for Mess!" responded our landlady, "and I have just found it! Really, it won't do. It isn't fair. It is worse than a nursery."

"My dear Mrs Hudson," said Holmes, rather more tartly, though with a suggestion of a wink in my direction, "my work has saved thrones and prevented war. Must I *really* be berated for the occasional litter that falls in my wake?"

"Well" sighed the object of Holmes's bombast, "I've never saved a throne but I have saved the box-file you tipped a full teapot into last week. Is that the one?"

"You have the Ms then?" I asked with some amusement.

"I have. The papers are stained with Darjeeling but they are dry and readable. I have had them strung, drying about my range for several days. Do you want them back now then?"

* * *

Within a few minutes Holmes was working again with the papers; now stiff, parchment coloured sheets following their immersion in the detective's tea. I marvelled more at the transformation of Holmes himself, from playful companion to earnest researcher. Seemingly oblivious of my presence, he was utterly absorbed in his quest. His long fingers darted like a pianist's through the cuttings and notes, his gimlet eyes resting briefly and then moving on as he searched the bundles of paper.

At last he snatched up a long, thin cutting which he held rigid in his fingers. Even from my chair a few feet away, I could see that it was not one of the London 'papers familiar to me.

Holmes's uncanny ability to sense my thoughts once again proved accurate. "It is from the *Manchester Guardian* some two and a half years ago," he remarked, passing me the cutting. "That paper is not, I admit, my usual reading matter but you know my love of the bizarre and *recherché*. A brief and unsatisfactory account of a Lancashire case in one of our London 'papers led me to seek out a version of the story from nearer home."

The cutting preserved several column inches. Despite Holmes's expectant look, I scanned the report with mounting disappointment.

> COTTON BROKERS' CLOSURE FOLLOWING INSURANCE SETTLEMENT
> ------
> *The Northern Bastion Insurance Company today settled in full the insurance claims brought by Mr Silas Moffat resulting from the disappearance and presumed death of his partner Mr William Jones.*
> *Readers will recall the mysterious disappearance of Mr Jones from the London express last February. The partners had been subject to threats of violence from former business associates in Italy and several Balkan countries, where they had once owned textile mills and dye-works.*

> *The involvement of local police had failed to protect the company or, after the event, to produce either the missing partner or any sign of the perpetrators.*
>
> *Having heard affecting evidence from Mr Moffat and clear testimony from Inspector Galloway of the Salford Police, who had been approached by Jones on the eve of his disappearance, the Northern Bastion Insurance declined to contest the case further and settled Mr Moffat's claim in full.*
>
> *The sum involved was not disclosed but is believed to be in excess of £10,000.*

I looked quizzically at my friend.

"You see nothing to perturb you there, Watson?"

"Nothing at all," I replied. "A distressing case of police negligence perhaps and mean spiritedness from the insurers."

Holmes nodded and held out his hand for the cutting. "On the face of it, Watson, you may be right. But are you not troubled by the details? The name of the disappearing partner? Italy and the Balkans? And more than anything – if all is so cut and dried, why the Bastion should decline to pay up?"

Holmes smiled and with a swift glance at his watch, proceeded to sweep up more of the litter that festooned the furniture of the sitting-cum-consulting room.

"Pray resume your seat, Watson, and do me the honour of hearing out a visitor whose cab I believe I hear outside even now. We shall give nothing away and I think you will be interested to hear what brings Mr Silas Moffat to our door…"

* * *

I had barely time enough to recover from the shock of Holmes's announcement before Mr Silas Moffat himself was shown into the room. Our visitor proved to be a stout, ruddy-faced man of perhaps fifty years, who walked stiffly, as though troubled in his joints, and puffed from the effort. He declined our settee and sank – though 'collapsed' might describe the descent more closely – into a chair before the window, declaring that he preferred a straight back and firm seat; being "a martyr to his back and knees." The skirts of his somewhat dusty frock-coat rose in a ruff about him and his luxurious beard and moustaches billowed in and out with his panting. For a minute or more Mr Silas Moffat sat in silence, save for his stertorous breathing, as he recovered from the exertions of his journey.

Holmes smiled indulgently and took post beside the fireplace, from whence he could both face his client and reach his tobacco. With a sweeping gesture Holmes begged our visitor both to be comfortable and to commence his tale.

"Mr Holmes, I am a frightened man. I fear for my life and that of my partner; Mr Edward Johnson. Through no fault of our own we are caught up in a desperate business. I doubt that you have heard of it but Edward Johnson and I are the sole shareholders of Sheffield Armour Plate. A small concern to be sure but one which was, until a month ago, marked for greatness. "

Holmes tapped his pipe against the grate and murmured encouragement.

"Yes, a month ago we secured (against the odds I might say) options on the sole supply of Bethlehem Steels' new armour plate throughout Italy and the Balkans. Think of that, Mr Holmes, Dr Watson. Think of the opportunities for shell proof steel for a re-arming Italy and throughout the Balkans; refortifying and defending all those disputed borders. Even at a mere penny for every pound ordered, Johnson and I could count on an early and comfortable retirement."

"*Could* count on…?" murmured Holmes.

"Precisely, my dear sir," puffed our visitor. "A week ago we began to receive threats. Threats to give up the business and abandon the Balkan contracts."

"What was the nature of these threats?" I asked.

"Ah, Dr Watson, there is the devilment of it. They were whispered at us from crowds, from amongst passengers on 'buses and in queues for trains. It is dastardly. No notes to trace or take to the police; just unnerving hints and 'accidents'. Why yesterday, a plant pot fell from my neighbour's house within feet of me and poor Johnson was *shoved* –there is no other word for it – into the path of a hansom. It is a miracle that he is alive now but he would not stay a moment longer in London and fled back to Sheffield this afternoon."

"So, what would you have me do?" asked Holmes abruptly and, I think, not a little impatiently.

"Well, sir, I…"

"I presume you have alerted the local police to your plight?"

"I have, sir, and they all but dismissed me as a foolish teller of tall stories."

Holmes tutted and shook his head. "Rest assured Mr Moffat, I do not make that mistake. Return to your lodgings and pack. Mrs Hudson will summon a cab and I urge you to rejoin your partner as soon as possible."

"Why, Mr Holmes, that is just the point. I am here to beg you to protect me and to see me safely aboard the eight-fifteen from St Pancras."

I could see from his reaction that the request came as a surprise, even to Sherlock Holmes. He tapped his pipe against his lips before answering with a shake of the head. "That I cannot do."

Moffat's face grew red with anger and his whiskers fair bristled annoyance. This petulant display was lost upon Holmes, however, as he smiled and extended his hand to our visitor.

"Alas, my dear Mr Moffat, urgent business will preclude my attendance upon you…though I will look into the matter for you, of course. Might I suggest though that Watson, here, accompany you? I can conceive of no better body-guard than Watson. He has left somewhere here his old service revolver and is possessed of an indomitable spirit, which will forestall even the most daring assassin I assure you. Leave with us your address in Sheffield and I shall be in touch."

* * *

I returned to Baker Street the following morning. The evening had proved one of the most disagreeable periods of my life – including those spent slung, wounded, across a mule in Afghanistan. My mood was scarcely improved by Holmes's broad grin as I accepted his welcoming glass of brandy and soda. It worsened, as he proceeded to chuckle and then laugh uncontrollably as I told my story.

"Holmes," I declared, "that man *deserves* to be assassinated. A meaner, more curmudgeonly rogue does not exist. Do you know, Holmes, *I* paid for our cabs this evening. *I* paid for a chop at the station and *I* carried the devil's luggage when a porter could not be found."

"Worse," I continued, "the fellow dawdled so much and argued so long over his hotel bill, that he missed the eight-fifteen."

"I thought he might" nodded Holmes.

"Did you? Well, you might have shared your views and saved me the need to spend an extra hour with the delightful Mr Moffat, buying him chops and porter and carrying his bags across St Pancras station."

Suddenly Holmes's laughter ceased and he sat upright. "An extra hour you say? How so? Surely there is a perfectly good stopping train to Sheffield at eight-thirty?"

"There is indeed," I sighed "but the admirable Mr Moffat would not take the risk of 'stopping'. He had taken a fancy to the ten-past-nine via Buxton."

"Buxton?" gasped Holmes.

"Aye, Buxton," I replied "I told him he was mad but Moffat would have it so. It would put 'them' off the scent, he said, and was a more comfortable ride."

"I shall remember the route should I ever have to travel that way" smiled Holmes.

"Will you?" I replied, "and I shall remember carrying a carpet-bag apparently filled with armour plate, from platform one to platform nine."

Again Holmes shot up in his chair, his fingers arched together and his face taut with mental activity.

"Platform nine…of course…it would have to be. Do you know, Watson, I believe we are pitted against no ordinary rogue here."

Whether Holmes would have said more I cannot say for a violent ringing at the front door heralded the arrival of a telegram. The telegram came from Edward Johnson, in Sheffield, alarmed that his friend was not aboard the train from London. His carpet bag had arrived but of Silas Moffat there was no sign.

The pressing business which, the previous evening, had kept Holmes from sharing my misery with Moffat seemed to have evaporated and so we made haste together to St Pancras Station. There Holmes visited the telegraph office before we caught an express to Sheffield, where we were met by Johnson and an Inspector Hakewill of the local police. We sat together in the waiting room, which was fortunately empty of other travellers.

Johnson was a tallish, thinnish fellow of about forty; clean-shaven save for a small moustache, which was waxed into upward curls at either end. He wore a tight, light checked suit and twirled a grey, derby hat in his hands as he talked. He spoke with a slight northern accent, in swift bursts as though he was loading and firing phrases from a gun.

"Poor Moffat", he began, shaking his head, "I begged him to come back here with me...safer up here, see...an assassin can hide in the crowds in London...but not up here. Not up here."

Hakewill flipped open his notebook and summed up the case, partly for our benefit and partly to allow us to correct or add details.

"Missed his train in London. You, Dr Watson, saw him safely aboard a later, less direct train; locked in a compartment which arrived up here at midnight, empty save for his bag and hat."

"His hat?" asked Holmes, "what size?"

The inspector flicked forward a page or two. "A black silk, size seven and three-quarters. Label from Kelway's of Sheffield but actually made in Manchester. That important is it, Mr Holmes?"

"It might convince a dubious juryman, Inspector."

Johnson sighed and rose to his feet. "I understand that my friend and partner, Silas Moffat, retained you, Mr Holmes, to protect his life. You signally failed. Failed in that duty...and now seem to think it appropriate...to assemble irrelevant data in an effort to conceal your own ineptitude. My friend's life was threatened. Threatened, I say...and you did nothing."

"On the contrary," responded Holmes coolly, "I devoted several hours to contemplation of your case – and that even before I met Mr Moffat. Watson will testify how deeply I delved into my archive of crime and the *outré*."

"You sat and smoked...and allowed my partner to go to his death…"

"I have seen no evidence that Mr Moffat is dead" replied my friend quietly.

A police constable approached us then and handed a telegram to Inspector Hakewill, who glanced at it before passing it to Holmes.

"What now?" demanded Johnson, his smooth face now showing signs of agitation.

"More data for the juror we spoke of earlier" replied Holmes and then, with a gesture towards Johnson, he added "Inspector, I advise you to secure this man. I can supply evidence which will see him convicted of at least two counts of fraud or attempted fraud."

"You're mad!" declared Johnson, his face red with anger.

"No madder than you, Johnson, for employing me as a pawn in your scheme of fraud and deception!"

The inspector nodded to his constable and each fastened tight upon one of Johnson's arms.

"It worked well enough in Manchester, when Silas Moffat lost his partner, Jones, that you thought you'd try it again in Sheffield. No insurance company likes the publicity of declining a claim which is backed by grieving friends and the police. Worse still for their investigators searching for evidence on a William Jones or an Edward Johnson. Perhaps next time you'd try John Smith, or is that too obvious perhaps?"

"What are you saying Mr Holmes?" stammered Hakewill, still firmly grasping Johnson. "Is all this an insurance fraud?"

"Indeed it is, Inspector", my friend replied, "Jones and Moffat were one and the same. Jones could easily disappear because he never really existed; or at least because he could only exist when Silas Moffat was absent. And now, we have Moffat missing because Johnson has appeared."

"But Moffat was a puffing, sick old man" I gasped "…a head shorter and quite a few pounds heavier than this fellow."

"Come Watson," riposted Holmes, "how often have you seen me lose an inch or two of height when I wanted, or put on a stone? It is the easiest thing in the world…and any actor could change his voice to order."

Holmes studied my face for a moment and then raised a finger. "Well, you are my doubting juror. Take up Johnson's hat. Tell me if it is the same size as Moffat's."

"Seven and three-quarters" muttered the inspector, still attached, limpet-like, to Johnson.

"It is" I stammered, beginning to see Moffat's jaw line in Johnson and the same shape of ear. "But how did Moffat get off that train. I put him aboard it myself."

"Why, Watson, the oldest trick in the book. Had it been a cab you'd have known in an instant. He boarded on one side and climbed out the other. He couldn't afford to take the express to Sheffield because it was in the centre of the station where all would see. The stopping train late at night has hardly anyone aboard and is at platform nine, up against the outer wall of the station. Nothing is easier than slipping out along that wall and away.

I daresay we shall find a barber near to St Pancras who shaved and trimmed the moustache of a thickset fellow on Tuesday night, before he boarded the last express of the night to Sheffield; just in time to meet the empty compartment of his 'friend' from Buxton."

"If your juror needs more, let me throw in this telegram. It is confirmation of a new policy from the Hallamshire Providential, of twenty thousand pounds, by an Edward Johnson on the life of his partner, Silas Moffat."

"Providential indeed" muttered the inspector, "this fellow's a criminal genius."

"Criminal for sure," snapped Holmes, "but no genius. Only a reckless fool would enlist me as a dupe in their scheme!"

The Steam Yacht *Pegasus*

I was surprised, on returning from a stroll one morning, to find my friend Sherlock Holmes in eager attendance on a plump, somewhat frumpish, though well-dressed lady of about fifty years. Without much thought I identified her as a cook or housekeeper, not from her costume (which was rather more costly and fashionable than I'd have expected from one in such a station) but from a remarkable resemblance to the smiling domestic whose cherubic countenance beamed out from a thousand advertisements for Bampton's groceries.

The lady sat bolt upright at our breakfast table, still with its litter of crumbs and crockery, while Holmes lounged in his chair. I had heard voices as I climbed our stairs and as I entered the room, Holmes sprang up and swept the morning's papers from my chair.

"Ah Watson!" cried my friend, "as timely as ever. Do come in. There is work to be done and your notebook and pencil will be needed. Sit my dear fellow. This is Lady Bampton. She has travelled overnight from Rainmouth to seek our help."

"Lady Bampton?" I queried, "I am sure I should know the name but…"

Our guest chuckled. "Yes dear, Timmy Bampton is my husband. I am the roly-poly party on all those red packets!"

"Of course!" I nodded my understanding. It was Timmy Bampton's red packets – of tea, biscuits, sugar, and almost every other item of grocery in daily use in a million kitchens each carrying the image of a cheery cook as a sign of their honest utility. 'Bampton's trustworthy groceries' were universal; a household revolution. Whereas every grocer would sell a quarter of loose tea, for a farthing extra the careful housewife could have a quarter of Bampton's Blend in its red packet. A guarantee of quality, freedom from adulteration and with a tiny photograph of a music hall star or politician of the day enclosed, gratis.

I studied Lady Bampton for a moment and did indeed recognise in her the cheerful figure whose rosy cheeks and tight curls decorated every one of Bampton's red packets.

"You know me now, don't you Doctor?" asked our visitor with a throaty chuckle. "If I'd brought my rolling-pin and apron, it'd have been easier wouldn't it?"

"Yes of course," I agreed "but what has happened to bring you here?"

"A bad business, Watson," responded Holmes. "Can you spare a day or two and travel down to Rainmouth with us. There is an excellent train from Paddington in fifty minutes. Bradshaw carries an advertisement for several agreeable hotels and there is just time to telegraph for rooms and to catch the train. We can hear the details as we travel down.

***

The four and a half hour journey to Kingsport, across the estuary from Rainmouth, passed swiftly. Lady Bampton proved an observant enough witness and, with careful prompting from Holmes, gave us a clear account of the events of the previous few days.

On Saturday, Sir Timmy Bampton had decided to try out his newly acquired steam yacht, the *SY Pegasus,* on a run down the coast from Cowes to Penzance. On the Isle of Wight, Bampton had run across an old friend, Captain Arthur Mills, the Polar explorer, who had agreed to join the party. He had also 'picked up' (according to Lady Bampton – who clearly did not entirely approve) the Chinese diplomat, Ho Chi Fat, and his companion, the noted Oriental linguist, Professor Lundy, who also came aboard.

The brief voyage was dogged by atrocious weather. Lady Bampton was clearly relieved, since although she was an excellent sailor and missed not a single meal; the others all kept to their cabins in some discomfort and distress. By Wednesday the storm had blown itself out and the yacht had put in at Rainmouth to pick up Sir Timmy's business partners, Oliver Tite and Sir Roland Dundas, and their wives, who had travelled down by train.

"We couldn't squeeze everyone aboard to sleep," explained Lady Bampton, as we sped past Reading, "so the Tites slept ashore but came out to us for the day trips and to dine."

We steamed up the estuary and around the coast, returning to the harbour with high tide to spend the night off Rainmouth Castle. The Volunteer gunners were practising with their guns and put on quite a show for us. Sir Timothy had a case of champagne rowed ashore for the officers and a barrel of beer for the men by way of thanks."

"That was the start of the trouble," continued Lady Timothy. The next day, Thursday, we were invited over to inspect the Castle. Do you know it?"

"Indeed I do", I replied. "It has a famous old tower at the centre. It is medieval I believe, and once beat off a Spanish galleon single handed with a pair of cannon. I understand there is a modern battery built alongside now, to protect the harbour from more heavily armoured modern foes."

"Yes" continued Lady Bampton, "there are four big guns. Very loud and smoky too. There is also the new experimental torpedo."

"Torpedo?" interrupted Holmes, his attention suddenly drawn from the window through which he had been staring until then.

"Yes, Mr Holmes. A nasty, stupid weapon."

"Indeed?"

"It was all Mr Tite's fault. Tite and Captain Mills. We were leaving the castle to return to the *Pegasus*, when Captain Mills leaned over the ramparts and pointed to a sort of slipway running out from beneath the sea-wall. The artillery lieutenant from the castle was a little embarrassed but made the best of it. It seems Rainmouth was chosen for trials of a new weapon, which is launched like a ship and runs out, guided by wires to hit any enemy warship trying to sneak into the harbour. I don't understand weapons and I don't want to. I was ready for tea but the gentlemen insisted on seeing this torpedo, so while Mrs Tite and I, with Mr Fat (who was not invited) and Professor Lundy went on into Rainmouth, the others scrambled down the rocks to see the torpedo battery."

"You did not witness what happened next then?" asked Holmes.

"I did not Mr Holmes. Oh, I wish I had. That stupid Mr Tite. Always trouble follows that man. If he wasn't arguing with Sir Roland, he was telling our crew how to manage the yacht or the soldiers how to fire their guns. An atrocious man! I wish my husband had never taken up with him."

"What did Tite do?" I asked.

"The men were watching the torpedo launch. Tite interfered in some way and the torpedo veered off course and hit our yacht! Oh, if only Tite could leave well alone!"

"Your yacht was torpedoed?" I gasped. "Was anyone hurt"

"Oh, bless you, Dr Watson, it was only a practice torpedo. It didn't explode but the silly thing stuck in the bows of *Pegasus* and we were stranded in Rainmouth for the night."

"Your husband had planned to move on, then?" asked Holmes.

"Oh yes. He had something important to tell his partners, Tite and Dundas, but he said he was determined to move on that evening. Now, of course, everything has changed. Oh, that wretched torpedo!"

Our train stopped briefly at Taunton and Holmes leant through the window of our compartment to buy a copy of every newspaper on the platform. He settled back into his seat and eagerly scanned the inner pages.

"Ah!" He suddenly declared, "the affair has reached the 'papers here. Lady Bampton, I fear your husband has been charged with murder."

I snatched up the *Somerset Evening Chronicle*, which lay on the seat beside Holmes and, as our train pulled out of Taunton, I read aloud the brief account which occupied barely more than a couple of inches of the national news on page two.

> *TRAGEDY ABOARD YACHT AT RAINMOUTH*
>
> *Reports have been received this morning of the death of the financier Sir Roland Dundas aboard the steam yacht of Sir Timothy Bampton in Rainmouth Harbour.*
>
> *The yacht arrived in the harbour on Wednesday evening and Sir Timothy and his guests, who are believed to include Captain Mills (who was recently presented with the Polar Medal by HRH the Prince of Wales) and the Chinese envoy Mr Ho Chi Fat, observed a display of gunnery by the Royal Devon Volunteer Artillery from the Castle.*
>
> *Later the same evening Sir Timothy entertained the party to dinner aboard his yacht. Sir Roland, who made his name and fortune through the introduction of tea planting to hitherto unexploited areas of Ceylon, and is believed to have been a major creditor of Bampton's, was later discovered dead at the foot of a companionway.*
>
> *The Devon Police have sought the assistance of Scotland Yard. The newly*

arrived Inspector Garner declined however to comment, beyond confirming that Sir Timothy Bampton was assisting with his enquiries.

Lady Bampton sank back into her seat and covered her face with her hands. I turned to Holmes, who tossed aside the other Taunton 'papers with a growl.

"Hah! So Garner declines to comment! We know better, eh, Watson? Garner is hardly Scotland Yard's finest. Why, faced with a teatime theft in the nursery, he would be more likely to arrest a rag doll or tin soldier than the child with strawberry jam all over its face! If he *has* arrested your husband, Lady Bampton, be assured it is almost proof of his innocence!

Our companion wiped her tear-stained cheeks and straightened her skirts. "Mr Holmes" she replied, "I have great confidence in you and Dr Watson but I have even more in my husband. My Timothy is not a murderer."

"Precisely so," replied Holmes with a smile, "but we must prove it; ideally by finding the real culprit. Are you ready to continue your story?"

"Of course, Mr Holmes, where was I?"

"At dinner on the yacht…" I suggested.

"Yes, at dinner. We were ten for dinner. Sir Roland and Lady Dundas, Captain Mills, Mr Fat and Professor Lundy were aboard with us. We sent the boat to fetch Mr and Mrs Tite and the officer from the battery, Lieutenant Hill. Also aboard the yacht were our cook, the four stewards, my maid, Lady Dundas's maid, my husband's man, John, and two members of the yacht's crew. Sir Timothy let the others go into Rainmouth with the main ship's boat. The two crewmen who stayed aboard were to row our visitors ashore later in the gig…I recall it was not a successful occasion."

"How so?" asked Holmes.

Lady Bampton seemed lost in thought for a moment. "I can't account for it. It was just the atmosphere. The food was excellent and we serve the finest wines, though neither my husband nor I partake you'll understand. No, it was the atmosphere. Captain Mills worked hard with tales of the Arctic and even Lieutenant Hill and Professor Lundy, neither of whom I fancy are naturally inclined to table-talk, tried their best. Neither Oliver Tite nor Sir Roland Dundas seemed relaxed and that frightful Chinaman simply watched us all evening. Oh, I tremble to remember it all."

"We remained together in the saloon when the gentlemen had their port; there simply isn't a room large enough aboard *Pegasus* for the ladies to withdraw. Instead, the two officers and Sir Roland went out onto the deck to smoke their cigars. It was a dark night and there was no moonlight to cheer us. Yet they remained together, on deck, until it was time for the shore party to leave."

"How do you know?" asked Holmes. "If you remained in the saloon and the night was so dark?"

"I could see the three glowing tips of their cigars. I should say all three leaned over the rail beside the wheelhouse. At one point one threw his cigar out into the harbour; it made a red arc like a shooting star. Lady Dundas saw it too and commented on it. I recall that it took a full quarter of an hour for us to explain the remark to Mr Fat."

Holmes nodded his approval. Our train clattered through Tiverton without stopping. Holmes leaned closer to Lady Bampton and I knew from his voice that we were reaching the key point in her story.

"Where was Dundas when the others came to leave?"
"He was closeted with my husband. I saw our guests off, which was not like Sir Timothy. He is usually a most considerate and attentive host."
"Indeed," nodded Holmes "but the others, where were they?"

"Professor Lundy came to the rail with me. Lady Dundas had retired to bed and the Chinaman remained in the saloon I think. I did not see Captain Mills. He had retired to bed too perhaps."

"When did your husband rejoin the party?" I asked.

"He didn't; at least not before I retired to bed. Shortly after eleven I heard him send for whisky and soda for Sir Roland and perhaps half an hour after that I heard my husband send John and the last steward to bed. The others had all retired by then."

"When did your husband retire?" I asked.

"I cannot say. We have never adopted the habit of separate rooms but he told me that his business with Sir Roland kept him up so late that he feared he would disturb me if he then came to bed and so finally snatched a few hours' sleep under a blanket on the couch in the saloon. All because he did not wish to disturb me. Had he been less considerate, with my evidence, he would not now be lying in Rainmouth's police station."

"As things turned out, I slept soundly that night and did not wake until after daylight, when the crew returned from Rainmouth and found Sir Roland's body at the foot of the companionway. My husband commanded that nothing was to be touched and immediately sent the boat back ashore to fetch the police."

"But he probably slipped," I cried. "There may be no case to answer and your husband, newly freed, will meet us from the train."

"I fear not, Dr Watson," replied Lady Bampton, her eyes downcast and once again welling up with tears. "For one thing, Sir Roland's throat had been cut and for another, my husband's shirt-front was smeared with his blood. He said he imagined it came from turning over the body but the police put quite another construction on the matter. I know my husband is innocent, I'm sure of it, but it all looks so dreadfully bad!"

***

Our train was ten minutes late pulling into Kingsport, where a sudden squall flecked our windows with rain drops. Nevertheless, a grim party awaited us beneath umbrellas and oilskins, upon the exposed platform. As Holmes stepped from our carriage, turning to offer his hand to Lady Bampton, our old sparring partner, Inspector Garner stepped forward.

"Well, Mr Holmes…you've had a long, wasted journey this time. I've never seen so tight-shut a case."

The Scotland Yard detective then ordered one of the local constables to take care of our travelling companion, while he retired with us to the waiting room. Fortunately, the room was empty as no trains were due for another hour or more.

"Mr Holmes", Garner began, "I don't mind your involvement in this case – it is Lady Bampton's prerogative to bring in outside help – and my sergeant will give you a copy of the witness statements we've already taken but I won't have you interfering with those witnesses, nor getting in my way. One sniff of obstruction and I'll have you in a cell. So be warned!"

Sherlock Holmes remained silent for a few seconds and then replied, quietly: "Inspector Garner, I am retained by Lady Bampton because she believes her husband to be innocent. I have agreed only to *investigate* however and retain an open mind. I am on the side of truth and justice, as you should be, and have no desire either to impede you or to shield the guilty. In my last twenty cases, I have assisted the police in twelve. No fewer than seven times I have prevented a gross miscarriage of justice and, I might add, saved Scotland Yard from both censure and ridicule.

I am here now in the spirit of cooperation. However, I see that we are to be rivals. Well, so be it! I trust that *you* will not seek to obstruct me?"

I glanced at Inspector Garner, whose normally florid countenance was now a flaming, apoplectic scarlet. He stood in the centre of the small waiting room, his waterproofs still dripping and his mouth silently working as though his indignation had outdistanced his vocabulary.

At last, he wagged his finger at us: "See here," he said, "and the same goes to you Dr Watson, one step out of line and…and…"

***

Holmes turned up his coat collar as we left the waiting room. He gestured back towards the inspector and murmured "Well, we can expect little further help from that quarter, Watson. Clearly, I have ruffled his feathers too often in the past."

"I presume we should find a boat to take us out to the yacht?" I asked.

"No, Watson, I think the battery should be our first port of call. I had better explain my intentions to Lady Bampton and then we shall seek out this Lieutenant Hill."

We took the ferry over the harbour to Rainmouth. I revelled in the fresh West Country air while Holmes studied the evidence already gathered by Inspector Garner. Fortunately, the rain had stopped and a milky sunshine was beginning to give hope of fairer weather, as we strolled along the front towards the castle and battery.

The approach to the castle was blocked by a narrow, yet very deep rock-cut moat. Fortunately, however, the forbidding aspect of the granite defences, which were rendered even greyer and grimmer than normal by the rain, was instantly belied by the cheery greeting of the blue-coated sentry. Leaning upon his carbine, the gunner listened to our request and then pointed out a small, single-storied hovel, which nestled against the medieval tower at the centre of the defences.

"Lieutenant Hill will be in there sir. That passes for the officers' mess here."

We found the Artillery Volunteers' lieutenant alone in the hut. He had clearly just eaten a solitary meal of bread and cheese and invited us to share the jug of local cider, which had washed it down.

Holmes shook his head. "We are here to avert a miscarriage of justice and must use our time well. Would you show us the torpedo, just as you demonstrated it to the party from the yacht?"

The lieutenant blushed and stammered his regrets: "Ah, no. I shouldn't have shown it off then and I really must not compound my fault by doing so again."

"Not even if it would save an innocent life?"

"You believe it has a bearing on this case, then?"

"Indubitably," replied my friend, "matters may seem bleak for Sir Timothy but I am beginning to form an alternative case and an understanding of the workings of your torpedo, with your account of events, will assist me materially. If you have any doubt of our integrity, I might add that my friend and colleague, Dr Watson, has seen active service with the Army Medical Department…"

"Attached to the Northumberland Fusiliers," I interjected.

"…Whilst I" continued Holmes, "have, on several occasions, been retained by Her Majesty's Government."

"You are right, of course" replied the Lieutenant. "Please follow me and I will show you exactly what I showed Sir Timothy's party."

We marched across the castle's small courtyard and through a narrow gate into a passageway, loop-holed for musketry, which snaked around the base of the medieval tower. The passage finally opened out onto a small gun platform, which mounted three antiquated muzzle-loading guns. These the lieutenant slapped with affection and declared the pride and joy of the Royal Devon Artillery. From that battery we also had our first clear view of the Steam Yacht *Pegasus,* moored perhaps one cable's length out in the channel.

We did not linger long however, as the lieutenant bade us follow him down a flight of stone steps almost to sea-level. In the shade of the castle and battery, the torpedo platform which we had now reached was cold and dank. There was a small wooden hut, with a pair of fine wires leading, strained and taut, down a narrow slipway and directly to the yacht. I tested one of the wires with my foot. It was little more than a piano wire, which thrummed as the sole of my boot slid across it. At the end of those wires we could just make out a red and white painted torpedo, lodged firmly in her bows.

"What went wrong?" I asked; I hope kindly.
"Not a thing," replied the lieutenant. "Well, not really. I launched one torpedo perfectly and recovered it without mishap. You see, the design is that should an enemy vessel be fool enough to try to enter the harbour, we can launch a torpedo down the slipway. These fine wires are fed out of the two drums over there as the torpedo goes and by slowing one or other of them, we can make the torpedo veer to left or right."

The Lieutenant mopped his brow. Clearly the remembrance of the demonstration was something of a trial. "I explained that quite clearly to everyone, yet Mr Tite still seems to have misunderstood and applied the brake to the wrong drum. He sent the torpedo smack into the yacht. It hasn't done any serious damage but it'll be another day before the Navy people come up from Weymouth to make good. *Pegasus* will be fine but I don't think my career will ever recover…"

"You are certain that your explanation of the torpedo's workings could not have been misunderstood?" asked Holmes.

"Yes, positively."

"And you are certain that it was Mr Tite, not Dundas or any of the others who interfered with the brake?"

"I am, though I shall be blamed, I am sure of that too."

"Never mind" I reassured him, "it'll all be forgotten in a month or two."

We turned to ascend the stone steps once more, leaving the forlorn artilleryman at the hut. Half way up, Holmes turned and called down to him: "Do you keep a watch on the harbour at night?"

"We do. Two sentries. A match-stick couldn't pass the castle without our knowing it."

"Capital," replied Holmes, "and I daresay no boat passed from shore to yacht, beside those taking the crew and later the diners ashore?"

"Inspector Garner asked the same question, Mr Holmes."

"Did he now?" replied Sherlock Holmes, tapping my arm, "and what was your answer?"

"Not a single boat passed all night besides those two. If any boat had crossed between yacht and shore, we'd have seen him. I wish they had for Sir Timothy's sake…but I can assure you they didn't."

***

Holmes and I walked in silence into Rainmouth. Eager as I was to confer with him, I knew better than to interrupt my friend's train of thought. I could tell that he was carefully assimilating the evidence we had just heard. It was all the more astonishing to me therefore when he suddenly called out to a fisherman, who was attending to his nets on the quayside.

"A good catch?"

"Not too bad sir…for the time of year."

"Excellent. Tell me, please, at low tide, could I walk out to that yacht yonder?"

"Walk out sir? Not a hope; the harbour's all mud thereabouts. It must be ten foot deep and sticky as toffee when the sea's off it." As though to prove the point, he seized a large pebble and tossed it out towards the yacht. The pebble landed with a 'plop' and immediately vanished beneath the sickly, yellow mud."

Holmes walked on in silence. At the town police station, we found Sir Timothy sitting in the Police Sergeant's kitchen, enjoying a plate of hot buttered toast, washed down with a mug of his own 'red-packet' tea. He could offer no explanation of either the death of Sir Roland or how his own shirt-front came to be smothered with blood.

"I had an amicable and perfectly satisfactory meeting with Sir Roland. Many years ago, he and Mr Tite had financed my first commercial ventures. For a quarter of a century, they have profited greatly by my hard work and success. We have all grown wealthy and I am still grateful for their early faith in me."

"However, after twenty-five years it seemed to me that the time had come to invoke a clause in the original contract which would permit me to buy my silent partners out of the company. My dear wife has probably told you that we invited the Dundases and Tites down here for some sight-seeing and a pleasant cruise around the Cornish coast."

"I regret to say that, in truth, my invitation *was* rather more of an ambush than might meet the eye but in business, it does sometimes help to spring the odd surprise…"

Bampton chuckled like a naughty schoolboy and bit deeply into his toast, the jam dribbling from the corners of his mouth as he smiled to himself. I glanced at Holmes, who caught my look and raised his eyebrows in acknowledgement.

"As a matter of fact, I needed only Dundas's agreement, or Tite's for that matter, since it required only a simple majority of the three of us to dissolve the partnership."

"I broached the subject with Tite as we were shown over the castle but he was most uncooperative about it. I feared a similar rebuff from Sir Roland last night but I offered generous terms and he agreed. It would have given me clear control of my own firm at last but we hadn't signed when we parted and now I have no idea what will become of his shares."

"Why did you not sign?" asked Holmes.

"It was late and both Sir Roland and I were tired. Besides, I have an idea he thought it only fair to explain himself to Tite too before he signed away their power over the company."

"Can you offer no explanation of the blood on your shirt?" I queried.

"None at all, I fear gentlemen. I was quite exhausted by so long and busy a day. I was loath to disturb my wife and so settled myself to sleep on the couch in the saloon. It was warm there and surprisingly comfortable and I am afraid I slept deeply and soundly until the commotion of the morning. I can only add that I know nothing whatsoever of Sir Roland's death."

***

Sherlock Holmes did not speak of the mystery again until we were seated in the yacht's gig, being rowed out across the harbour.

"Quite a puzzle, Watson; well worth the long journey from Baker Street. Bampton hardly seems as reckless a murderer as Inspector Garner would have us believe, yet who else on board would wish to murder Sir Roland, or could have reached the yacht, unseen by Lieutenant Hill's eagle-eyed sentries, across two hundred yards of either glutinous mud or fast-flowing tidal water?"

"The crew perhaps?" I ventured.

Holmes smiled. "The two crewmen slept together in their quarters and have vouched for each other. Besides, what motive could they have"?

"The Chinaman then? Or the professor…what was his name, Lundy?"

"No, Watson. They too shared a cabin and are also without a motive for murder."

"You surely cannot believe that one of the ladies, or Captain Mills, the hero of the Polar ice, could have cut Dundas's throat?" I gasped.

"No Watson, I do not."

"Or Bampton's man, John?"

"Hardly."

"But Holmes, it must have been one of those left on board the yacht that night and how often have you told me that when the impossibilities are eliminated, it is the improbable which must be the truth?"

"Indeed Watson," replied my friend, "either that or one of the impossibilities is not impossible!"

Our boat bumped gently then against the hull of the yacht and we ascended the short boarding ladder to the deck. Holmes inspected both the steps where Dundas had been found and the saloon, where Bampton had slept on the night of the murder.

"There is nothing for us here, Watson," remarked my friend with a sigh. "Someone has had every trace of victim and murderer washed from the scene. I imagine we must thank our Scotland Yard inspector for that."

Our attention was seized then by a swish of silk. We turned, expecting to greet one of the ladies, but instead the

Chinese diplomat, Ho Chi Fat, appeared from the door to the cabins below deck. Professor Lundy soon also appeared and seemed relieved to have found us.

"Ah, Mr Holmes and Doctor Watson," he said in a whisper. "The Inspector wishes to speak to us all in the saloon but Mr Fat" (to whom he nodded) "was most anxious that you have a piece of information before it is too late."

Holmes bowed slightly to the Oriental and spoke a few words in his native tongue. Mr Fat seemed delighted and gabbled away earnestly. Holmes raised his hands in gentle protest and explained through Lundy that "I have only a few phrases of greeting or conventional conversation; I fear we shall still require interpretation."

Lundy too bowed and explained to his friend. He then proceeded to elucidate: "Mr Fat was one of the first to see the body of Sir Roland Dundas. He has a medical qualification and sought at first to help. However, it was immediately obvious, he says, that Dundas had been dead for some hours. So, instead, he proceeded to examine the area around the body. Mr Fat says that he is a keen student of yours Mr Holmes and hopes to introduce some of your methods to Canton, when he returns there."

Holmes smiled to himself and then bowed again to Mr Fat, who returned the compliment.

"Everything was as Inspector Garner's report no doubt shows," continued Lundy, "except for one small detail. There were several pools of water on the deck, almost in a discernable trail towards the bows of the yacht."

"But it had been pouring with rain. The whole deck must have been soaking wet" I ejaculated.

"Yes, yes, indeed," replied Lundy. "But Mr Fat says that the water was salt. It was sea water, Dr Watson."

Mr Fat nodded vigorously and repeated what I took to be the Chinese word for salt or salt water.

"But how could you possibly know that?" I asked.

"Mr Fat tasted it" replied Lundy.

"Capital!" exclaimed Holmes and he shook Mr Fat's hand.

"So, Watson, there it is. Your impossibility must be possible!"

We hurried then to the saloon, where Inspector Garner was questioning Bampton's manservant, John. As we entered, Garner turned to us with an air of triumph. He slapped a small sheet of paper down upon the table. "There, Mr Holmes, I don't think Sir Timothy Bampton will wriggle out from under this."

Holmes picked up the paper. It was a single page of 'SY Pegasus' headed paper, containing part of a letter, or note, from Bampton to Oliver Tite. In what both his wife and Professor Lundy admitted was Sir Timothy's characteristic scrawl, Holmes read aloud a passage containing the damning phrase, "at all costs I must be rid of you and Dundas…"

"It hardly proves anything," I objected.

"It is *motive* enough for any jury" sneered the Inspector, with an air of triumph. "We have only Sir Timothy's word for Sir Roland's amicable agreement to dissolution of the partnership. What if Dundas *actually* refused to agree? It may be that you have had a lucky escape, Mr Tite, since it would appear that Sir Timothy would stop at nothing to be rid of you!"

I might have argued further had Holmes not caught my eye with a subtle shake of his head. We were distracted then by a gasp from Lady Bampton, who sobbed deeply and collapsed back into a chair. The inspector smiled smugly at Holmes and declaring that his work was done, offered us a seat in his boat back into Rainmouth.

To my utter surprise Holmes agreed and he strolled with the inspector and Tite to the taffrail, below which the police rowing boat was tied. As we were rowed ashore by Garner's two constables, I was surprised to hear Holmes in idle conversation with Oliver Tite. If anything, Tite was even more surprised than I and clearly answered with some resentment.

"What gorgeous air, Mr Tite," said my friend, throwing back his head and breathing in deeply through his nostrils. "Fill your lungs!"

"I shall breath normally Mr Holmes," responded Tite acidly, "if anything, the air is too full of the scents of decaying fish and seaweed for my liking."

"Ah, but the ozone. Take in the ozone."

Tite sighed and looked out to sea, away from Holmes. My friend was not to be put off however and to my astonishment, tapped Tite's arm and asked another question.

"Do you swim, Mr Tite? It is the healthiest and best of exercises. The counting house may be profitable but it is not healthy."

"I do not swim, Mr Holmes. I *cannot* swim."

Then Garner leaned forward, his face lit by another sneering grin. "I see where we're going, Mr Holmes. I've been there myself…but it's quite true; Mr Tite can't swim a stroke. While the others bathed, he stayed aboard the *Pegasus* and watched."

We sat in silence for the rest of the journey ashore. I was surprised again by Holmes when we were at last tied up at the dock, as he suddenly pushed in front of Mr Tite to ascend the ladder first. I was even more astonished when, as he reached the uppermost rung, Holmes's foot slipped and he butted Tite backwards into the harbour.

We froze as Tite plunged into the water, his arms raised above his head and his mouth wide open as though in a silent cry of horror. For nearly half a minute we stared at the water, where a trace of bubbles and Tite's straw hat, were all that marked the place of his descent.

A second more and Inspector Garner pulled himself together enough to order both his men into the water. A minute passed before they had shed their boots, helmets and tunics and dived together into the grey-green water.

To our relief Tite was shortly after raised from the depths and efficiently 'pumped out' by the two capable policemen. Garner watched in silence but as Tite was packed into a trap and hurried away towards the cottage hospital, he drew alongside Holmes. His voice was little more than a hiss, yet I still heard the inspector's threat: "If I could prove, Mr Holmes, that your little demonstration there was anything more than an unfortunate accident, I should not hesitate to charge you with attempted murder! Let this be an end of the matter. Accept defeat and go home!"

I stared at Holmes. Surely he could not deliberately have risked Tite's life just to see if he could really swim? I said nothing but, as so often before, he knew my thoughts.
"Come Watson, do not judge too harshly. This case is dark, very dark indeed. Yet how often, Watson, have we found (like Fuller) the night to be darkest just before the dawn?

***

Holmes said nothing more of the case over dinner at our hotel and suggested an early night. I was happy to agree and we parted at a little after half-past ten. I was tired and sunk in gloom but Holmes seemed strangely excited as he strolled away down the corridor.

The following morning Holmes was positively jovial at breakfast. He lingered long over both kipper and bacon, chirruping to the serving girl and chatting inconsequentially to me. At last, when I fancied the meal over, he further astonished me by ordering a fresh pot of tea, with the explanation that "the inspector will wish to have a cup with us!"

I opened my mouth in protest but Holmes raised a finger to his lips and nodded towards the door of the breakfast room, where indeed stood Inspector Garner and his two faithful constables. Holmes stood and offered the Scotland Yarder a seat.

"I trust this *is* important," growled the inspector. "I meant what I said about any further nonsense."

"Oh, inspector" replied my friend, "you judge me too harshly. I wish both to report *and* solve a crime for you."

"Oh yes," responded Garner, with some impatience. "What crime would that be?"

"Why? Theft of course. No doubt the owner of the stolen goods will soon report the matter herself." Holmes then summoned the maid and whispered some instructions. While Garner drank his tea and continued to growl his threats, she vanished and then returned, bearing a cone-shaped, brown paper parcel in her arms. Holmes took the parcel and placed it upon our table.

Garner and I stared at Holmes awaiting an explanation. He smiled at us and began slowly to peel away the wrappings of the parcel.

"The crime, Inspector Garner, is the theft of this object. In returning it to you, I solve both the theft and the murder of Sir Roland Dundas." So saying, Holmes tore away the brown paper to reveal a small ship's bell. Around the rim of the shining, brass bell were the letters: "S. Y. PEGASUS".

At the same moment another constable came racing into the breakfast room. He saluted the inspector as though about to make his report, yet said not a word. Rather, he stood, open mouthed, staring at the bell.

"Well, man," snapped Garner, "what is it? Has the whole town gone mad?"

The constable wiped his brow: "Word's come from the 'Pegasus, sir…someone has stolen their bell…"

Holmes smiled his thin smile. "I suggest you return the bell whence it came," he said icily. "I fancy it was rung last at midnight but could not be found to signal the first watch of the morning. You might ask Lieutenant Hill whether his sentries saw the thief and his boat approach the yacht during the night. If they did not, you might consider the implications of that for the night of the murder; and feel free to return here for an explanation. Until then, good-day to you, inspector."

Holmes and I remained at our table, surrounded by the litter of our breakfast and the paper wrapping of the bell. The bell itself was carried off under the arm of Garner's police messenger.

"Holmes" I gasped, as soon as we were alone, "what does it all mean?"

"Is it not obvious, Watson?" he replied. "Come now, the facts of the case are clear enough. Either someone aboard the 'Pegasus' murdered Sir Roland Dundas, or the murderer came out to the boat and returned ashore after the deed was done. Mr Fat's pool of salt water rather suggests that someone climbed aboard does it not?"

"Now, if Tite is our murderer (and I was sure of it from the start) then he must have found a way of reaching the yacht, and returning ashore, which was invisible to the keen-eyed sentries at the Castle. The current at high tide would be too much for all but the best swimmer and the mud at low tide, as we saw, would prevent a diver, say, from wading out."

"Could he not have approached from the Kingsport side?" I asked.

"A good point, Watson, but as Garner records in his notes there are no boats to be had on that side of the estuary downstream of the ferry and in any case, the height of the castle gives the sentry there a complete view of the harbour, even beyond the moored yacht."

"I take it that you stole the bell, Holmes, and I see why. But how on earth did you reach the yacht unseen?" I asked.

"The same way Mr Tite did."

"But you proved he cannot swim…unless you are suggesting he would be willing to risk near certain death to preserve his alibi?"

"No, Watson, I believe my experiment was a satisfactory one. Tite did not swim out to the yacht…and nor did I to steal the bell."

"Then how?"

"The torpedo, my dear Watson. I cannot tell whether Tite sent it into the yacht deliberately, or whether having accidentally diverted it, he saw the possibilities of the guiding wires; but it scarcely matters. You have seen how the torpedo is guided to its target by two thin wires. They are tiny, yet immensely strong, and they are taut, still, between the shore and the yacht, whose bows they pierced. You struck a note on them yourself, if you recall, just like plucking the string of a banjo!"

"I have proved, by taking the bell, that it is quite possible to cross from the torpedo battery, inching your way along the wires, keeping just my head above the seawater. They do not have to take your weight Watson, just to guide you to the yacht. Even a non-swimmer like Tite could float out, perhaps using a life-preserver, steadying and steering himself by the wires. A swimmer might be swept out to sea by the tide but by clinging to the wires, he could pass safely to and fro. I did not swim a yard Watson, yet I stole away with the ship's bell in a bag around my neck. I crossed unseen, Watson, and so did Tite. I am certain of it."

We waited in vain however for Inspector Garner. By one o'clock it was clear he would not return to us. Instead we sought him out. At the police station, Holmes left me outside as he enquired within for the Scotland Yarder.

He returned with a snort of rage and disappointment. "Watson," he declared, "my theatricality has been my undoing! It seems Tite was on the quay, when the boat from the yacht came ashore with news of the theft of the bell. Tite must have seen in an instant that all was up. Ah! Watson! What a foe that man is!"

"But where is he now", I queried, "and where is Garner?"

"Garner has set off across country. Tite hired a dog cart from his hotel saying he was going for a ride over the moors. The driver was found unconscious by the roadside an hour ago and Tite has vanished with the cart. The police think he'll make for either Weymouth or Plymouth and have telegraphed to their colleagues in those towns. Just as likely he'll try for the main railway line north. In any case, it is Garner's problem now…Ah! Here is Sir Timothy, fresh from his luncheon with the sergeant's wife. Perhaps we should stroll down to the yacht with him."

In the days that followed, I followed the progress of the pursuit through the newspapers. Holmes declined to be drawn further into the matter; I suspect hoping that Garner would be forced to swallow his pride and to seek my friend's assistance. A fortnight passed and no further developments were reported, beside the futile attempts of the police to close all ports to the fugitive.

At length I remonstrated with Holmes, arguing that it was his public duty to offer advice –if he knew or suspected something that Garner did not. He turned instead to his violin, offering only one comment; that he had been employed solely to prove Sir Timothy Bampton's innocence and that having done so, his involvement was at an end.

Also from MX Publishing

MX Publishing is the world's largest specialist Sherlock Holmes publisher, with over a hundred titles and fifty authors creating the latest in Sherlock Holmes fiction and non-fiction.

From traditional short stories and novels to travel guides and quiz books, MX Publishing cater for all Holmes fans.

The collection includes leading titles such as *Benedict Cumberbatch In Transition* and *The Norwood Author* which won the 2011 Howlett Award (Sherlock Holmes Book of the Year).

MX Publishing also has one of the largest communities of Holmes fans on Facebook with regular contributions from dozens of authors.

www.mxpublishing.com

Also From MX Publishing

London, 1920: Boston-bred Enoch Hale, working as a reporter for the Central Press Syndicate, arrives on the scene shortly after a music hall escape artist is found hanging from the ceiling in his dressing room. What at first appears to be a suicide turns out to be murder . . .

The first in the Enoch Hale trilogy including *'The Poisoned Penman'* and *'The Egyptian Curse'*.

www.mxpublishing.com

Also from MX Publishing

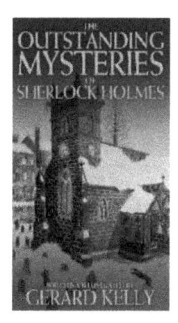

Our bestselling short story collections 'Lost Stories of Sherlock Holmes', 'The Outstanding Mysteries of Sherlock Holmes', 'Untold Adventures of Sherlock Holmes' (and the sequel 'Studies in Legacy') and 'Sherlock Holmes in Pursuit'.

www.mxpublishing.com